Tasha's Christmas Wish

A Christmas Adventure

Frances Wong

Frances Wong

To Dad
For all his support.

Chapter 1

The Easter Bunny

Meeting a magical creature is a lot more difficult than you'd think but Tasha was never one to give up.

She didn't dare move, she wouldn't even blink. As still as a statue, as quiet as a mouse, she sat in absolute silence. She stared through the patio doors into her back garden, waiting. Bushes lined the walls, flowers bobbed in the breeze as the sun slowly rose into the sky turning the clouds to a dreamy shade of pink.

Tasha wasn't sure how long she'd been waiting but it'd been dark when she crept downstairs. Ignoring the TV and even her toys, she had settled in front of the patio doors and waited. It wouldn't be long now.

"Watcha doing?" asked Billy, her brother, as he made his way into the kitchen.

She yelped and almost fell off the kitchen stool. Quickly, she glared back into the garden. Nothing had changed. It was fine. She was okay. She breathed out, unable to forgive herself if she'd missed it.

Her brother wriggled his way past her and

pressed his nose up flat against the window. His breath fogged up the glass. "Has the Easter Bunny come yet? Have you seen it?"

"Not yet," Tasha grumbled.

"How long've you been waiting?"

"Ages."

Billy shuffled off. "Aw, well, never mind. Maybe you're too early?"

After last year, she was sure she'd get up in time to spot the Easter Bunny. Last year, she'd leapt out of bed, raced down stairs and found mum and dad having breakfast. She'd run past them but her heart had sunk to find brightly coloured chocolate eggs already dotted all over the garden. The Easter bunny had already visited.

"They were there when we woke up," Mum had explained.

Last year, Tasha had missed seeing the Easter Bunny but not this year. This time, she'd woken up early enough to see the Easter Bunny for herself, hopefully. All she had to do was wait. She didn't even look up when her brother scrunched his hand into a bag of sweets.

"Want one?" he garbled, mouth full of chewing.

"What am I going to do?" she asked, ignoring the sweet packet. It was before breakfast after all. "I'm too late, I'm too early. I'm never going to meet a magical person."

She wanted her wish more than anything. Her whole life would be better if her wish was granted. This was something huge, something so important she'd planned this moment for months!

"Have you thought about camouflage?" Billy suggested.

Tasha's brother Billy was good at everything. Okay, he farted – a lot – and he picked his nose. Once, Tasha had even seen him eat it! But, despite all that, Billy was amazing, much more amazing than she was. One time, when she was stuck with her homework, he did it in two seconds. And he could reach all the high cupboards where mum and dad kept the biscuits. He could even climb all the best trees. She couldn't do any of that! But, if she got her wish, she would.

"Great idea," she said thoughtfully. He did know *everything*. "Where does the Easter Bunny get the eggs from anyway?"

"He lays them," Billy said, knowingly. "Like an enormous, fury chicken."

She pulled a face and mumbled "Hmm," at him without taking her eyes off the garden.

This was her last chance to see a magical creature. She'd tried wishing on a star, she'd thrown a penny into a wishing well, she'd even wished on a fallen eyelash. None of it had worked so she was going straight to a magical person to ask them herself, if only she could find one.

"Ugh, I'm never going to see the Easter Bunny," she complained after waiting another five minutes that had felt like an eternity.

Billy grinned at her. It wasn't as reassuring as he thought but he said, "You will. If anyone's going to see the Easter Bunny, it's going to be you. You *never* give up!"

"Natasha, time to go upstairs and get dressed," said Mum, heading for the kettle. "Now, please."

"But, Mum! I can't!" she cried. "I'll miss the Easter Bunny. He or she," Tasha paused, thinking, "or *they* could be here any minute!" This was so unfair! How could Tasha go upstairs now when she was so close to seeing the real life Easter Bunny? What if she missed it? What if the Easter Bunny came and she didn't see it. This was a nightmare! She ground her teeth. "I've waited my whole life for this moment!"

Mum snorted into her steaming mug of coffee and took a large gulp before saying, "A watched Bunny never arrives."

"But Mum!" Tasha whined, "It's almost the time he came last year. I only need," Tasha looked up at the clock and whispered as she counted, "forty more minutes!"

This was a disaster. How could she ask her wish if the Easter Bunny left before she could speak to him. Her parents had no idea how vitally important this was.

Mum raised her eyebrows as she took another sip.

"Please, Mum," Tasha begged, "I just want to see one magical person. Just one. I haven't found any unicorns in the woods, there weren't any leprechauns in the hollow trees, I couldn't see any fairies anywhere near toadstools and there were no pixies on the moors when we went on holiday. The Easter Bunny is my *last chance*!"

Mum very thoughtfully took a slow and steady sip from her coffee.

"Fine," Tasha grumbled. "But if you see the Easter Bunny, call me straight away!"

"Will do."

No one in the history of the entire planet has ever got changed as fast as Tasha and in half a moment, she was back on the kitchen stool, fiercely glaring into the garden.

Much to her relief, there was no sign of the Easter Bunny, yet. *That was lucky*, she thought to herself. She hadn't missed it. A bubble of excitement tingled in her tummy. This was it, this was the day she was finally going to see the Easter Bunny in real life, in her garden, leaving eggs for her family. For real. And then, she could ask her wish.

She squealed.

"Breakfast time!" called Mum.

Tasha gobbled down her toast sitting on her stool while staring out into the garden. It wouldn't be long now. *A real Easter Bunny*, she thought to herself. *Amazing*! She grinned with excitement.

"Billy! Natasha!" Mum called, "Shoes on!"

"What!" Tasha couldn't believe it. Her heart sank. "But, Mum!" she cried.

"Not now, Natasha," Mum said with a sigh. "Billy has his climbing class and you know he has his tournament coming up. He can't afford to miss any classes, right now. Dad has to go into work, so you're coming with me."

She felt sick. Her lip wobbled. All her dreams were

slipping away.

"Come on, Tash," said Billy, trying to help. "If I win, you can hold the trophy. It's going to be amazing."

She couldn't give up, not when she was so close. "*Please*, Mum," she whispered,

Blinking away the prickle of tears, she knew it was no use. All she could do was go with Mum to Billy's climbing class and miss her chance to see the Easter Bunny, possibly forever.

Fuming, she sat at the back of the enormous hall her brother's class was in, leaning against the wall while Billy, wearing a harness, climbed the opposite wall. He was amazing at climbing. Tasha was wouldn't even try, she hated heights. Just the thought of climbing the wall, even with a harness, made her knees go wibbly.

A knot of worry and dread sank in her tummy. If only she hadn't gone to Billy's climbing class. *It's so unfair,* she grumbled to herself. She'd been so close. She'd almost seen a real magical creature. Maybe it wouldn't be too late. A tiny flame of hope burnt in her heart. Crossing her fingers, she wished and hoped that when she got home, she'd still have a chance to see the Easter Bunny and ask her wish. Maybe they'd be late this year. It was a slim chance but it was the only hope she had.

Billy's climbing instructor wandered over to Tasha with a friendly smile. "Hello there," she said, breaking Tasha from her thoughts. "You're Billy's sister, aren't you? Would you like to have a try climbing?"

Tasha gulped and her stomach flipped. The cliff shaped wall was enormous. She felt dizzy just looking at it. She firmly shook her head.

"Not today," she squeaked.

She did *not* like climbing. Even the thought of it made her dizzy and her knees wobble. Billy was a natural climber but Tasha couldn't even take one step!

"You never know what you're capable of until you believe in yourself," said the instructor. "Okay. Well, let me know if you change your mind."

Tasha did not change her mind.

Unfortunately, events were about to change her mind for her.

"I've got bad news, I'm afraid," said the climbing instructor at the end of the class. "Billy's partner has broken her leg and won't be competing in the tournament."

"Oh gosh!" Mum cried, "Let me call her mother."

As Mum drifted off, peering at her phone, the instructor offered Billy a sad smile.

"I'm afraid this means you're out the tournament too, Billy."

"What?" Billy gasped. Tasha gasped too. This was terrible! She saw her brother's eyes shimmering as tears gathered. "But, I've trained so hard."

"I know, I'm so sorry, Billy. You can't compete without a partner."

Tasha felt as if she was watching her brother's whole world crumble. She wished there was something she could do to help, something she could say. Her heart ached.

"Tasha can do it," Billy blurted.

"Wait, what?"

He glanced at her and went on, "Yeah, Tasha would be great! She can be my partner."

"Natasha, would you like to be Billy's partner for the tournament?"

She looked at his pleading eyes then up at the enormous wall that loomed over her, making her feel dizzy.

"Right, I'm back. What did I miss?" asked Mum, as she pushed her phone back into her bag.

"Natasha is going to be Billy's climbing partner."

Mum looked surprised. "Are you? I thought you didn't like climbing."

When Tasha replied, she knew in her heart what she said was the truth. "I want to help Billy." Now her wish was even more important. She *had* to get home before the Easter Bunny arrived.

His face burst into the most enormous, grateful smile she'd ever seen in all her life. His entire body drooped with relief.

"Well, it's not until after Christmas so we have some time."

That was lucky, because now she really needed her wish granted. If it wasn't, she'd never be able to help Billy with the tournament.

She looked up at the enormous climbing wall and gulped. This was going to be more difficult than she could handle.

As soon as she got home, she kicked off her shoes and raced through the house to the kitchen and the patio doors.

Dad was back from work. She almost knocked over his cup of tea as she zoomed through the living room towards the kitchen.

She hoped and crossed her fingers. She wished and wished that she wasn't too late, that she'd still have time. She'd been waiting years to see the Easter Bunny - all her life, in fact!

Sadly, the hopeful smile slipped from her lips. Her hands hung limply by her side. She was too late.

Glimpses of colourful, glittering eggs peeped out from under the bushes and trees all over the back garden. There was even one on her pink swing. All her hopes were obliterated.

The Easter Bunny had already visited.

Dad's heavy hand landed on her shoulder. "You alright kiddo? You look upset." He pushed open the patio doors. "Let's go have an Easter egg hunt, eh?"

Tears prickled at the corners of her eyes. She bit her lip. This was hopeless, she'd never be able to ask her wish. Without her wish, she'd never be brave enough to help Billy in his climbing tournament and that meant *everything*.

Billy nudged Tasha's side. "Don't worry," he said kindly. "There's always the Tooth Fairy."

A small smile crept across her lips. Her brother always had good ideas.

Chapter 2

The Tooth Fairy

Tasha crossed off the days on her calendar as the tournament quickly approached. Unfortunately, she was still no closer to asking her wish. The Tooth Fairy really was her last hope.

Each day, when Billy brushed his teeth, she ran into the bathroom to check if any were wobbly. Each day, she trudged back out as all his teeth stubbornly refused to wobble.

"How am I supposed to meet the Tooth Fairy if none of your teeth fall out?" she grumbled, offering her brother another sweet. Mum always said that eating too many sweets would make their teeth fall out. She really hoped Mum was right.

"How about your teeth?" her brother suggested. "You're old enough to lose a tooth, now. Most of mine have already fallen out."

Tasha thought about that. She ran her tongue around her teeth wondering how she could get just one, small tooth to fall out. All she needed was one, *just one*, white tooth but none of her teeth were wobbly.

"How do I get one to fall out?" she asked, thinking of all those times she'd seen Billy wobbling his teeth.

"You just have to wait."

She shook her head in disbelief. "Impossible."

The days dragged by slowly. The tournament got agonisingly close. It felt like an eternity of months and months until one wonderful, incredible, amazing day.

It was lunchtime at school. Tasha carried her rattling lunch tray to the table where she sat next to her best friend, Hafsa. She was just tucking into a shiny, red apple when one of her teeth felt a bit strange. She gulped down the apple and felt around her mouth with her tongue.

Within moments, she found the intriguing tooth and to her absolute amazement, the tooth wobbled. *Tasha had a wobbly tooth!* She couldn't believe her luck! This was fantastic, it was brilliant, it was about time! She leapt up into the air.

"I've got a wobbly tooth!" she shrieked across the school dining hall.

Everyone in the dining hall froze. On the other side, sitting at his table, Billy smiled.

All adult heads snapped round in Tasha's direction. She quickly lowered into her chair under the glare of every dinner lady scowling at her.

"I've got a wobbly tooth," she whispered to Hafsa with a huge grin on her face.

This was the best thing that had ever happened to her. Now, she would actually meet the Tooth Fairy, the real life Tooth Fairy. A tingle of excitement bubbled in her tummy. This time, she couldn't fail. The Tooth Fairy came at night, there was no chance she'd miss her now. She was going to stay up all night if she had to.

Unfortunately for Tasha, wobbly teeth don't fall out straight away. The tournament was fast approaching and she hadn't managed to ask her wish. She soon realised she'd have to wobble it out. She wobbled that tooth all morning long.

"Don't wobble your teeth at the table, kiddo," said Dad.

She wobbled her tooth sitting at her desk at school.

"Hands out your mouth, please, Natasha," ordered her teacher.

She wobbled her tooth while watching TV sat on the sofa.

"That looks so gross. Stop it!" Billy complained.

"You did it," Tasha snapped. "You used to wobble your teeth on the sofa all the time! Anyway, I need it to fall out. How did you make your teeth fall out?"

He thought for a moment. "I wobbled them. A lot. Are you trying to *catch* the Tooth Fairy?" he asked.

"No," explained Tasha, "I just need to talk to her, that's all. I need to ask her something." *My wish*, she thought.

He shrugged and looked back at the TV. She got back to wobbling her tooth. It wouldn't be long now.

The trouble with teeth is that they're stubborn little things. It had met is match with Tasha. Little did that tooth know, she *never* gave up.

She anxiously ticked off the days on her calendar as she waited for the day her tooth fell out.

It took an entire week, which is basically forever! By then, her new tooth had already started to poke through.

The tooth was hanging on by barely a thread when, all of a sudden, just like that, the small, white tooth tumbled out into Tasha's hand.

She dashed downstairs to show Billy and her mum and dad. She clutched the tooth tightly as she absolutely could not lose this tooth. This was her only chance.

"It fell out! It fell out!" she cried with excitement as she burst through into the kitchen.

"Oooh!" said Dad, "The Tooth Fairy's visiting us tonight!"

"Yes!" she shouted with a thump of her fist. She felt as if it was Christmas and her birthday all rolled into one. She could barely keep still, she was so excited.

It happened in an instant.

She had no idea how.

The tooth slipped out her hand and flew through the kitchen! It all happened in slow motion. Tasha's mouth dropped open in disbelief. All her dreams were disappearing away.

She gasped.

The smooth, white tooth crashed down onto the floor tiles, bounced, bounced and rolled. It was heading under the fridge where it would be lost forever!

All of a sudden, Mum's hand slapped down on the kitchen floor. Tasha's heart tightened. She hoped, really wished that Mum had caught the tooth. She crossed her fingers and whispered hopes under her breath.

There, gripped between Mum's thumb and finger was Tasha's tiny, white tooth. Her *first ever* lost tooth. She nearly shook with relief. It was all saved!

Mum helped her to wrap the tooth in a paper towel before she carefully slipped it under her pillow.

Now, all she had to do was wait.

That night, she pulled on her pyjamas, quickly brushed her teeth (and then brushed them again because Dad said she hadn't brushed them long enough) and, eventually, got ready for bed. She sat cross-legged on top of the duvet, eyes fixed on her pillow, under which the tooth was hidden.

Mum knocked gently on the door and peeped her head through. "Bedtime story?" she asked hopefully.

Tasha bit her lip. She wanted to say yes. She had a bedtime story every single night, without fail. It was her favourite part of the day. She wasn't sure if she could fall asleep without a story and she and Mum had got to a really good bit in the book they were reading. But she had a mission and it was important. It was for Billy.

"Not tonight, Mum," said she, brightly. "I'm waiting for the Tooth Fairy."

"Yes, of course," said Mum with a little smile, "I get so muddle headed, I forgot. Night night."

It was only a few moments later when Dad tapped on Tasha's door.

"Lights off?" he asked, "Or a bedtime story?"

She was tempted to have a quick bedtime story, but she didn't have time. The sooner the Tooth Fairy thought Tasha was asleep, the sooner she'd arrive.

"Maybe tomorrow," she told him with a smile.

"Night then," and Dad flicked off the light.

She was plunged into darkness and shadow but still, she didn't take her eyes off the pillow. Not even for a moment.

A small tap on the door made her jump.

"Tooth Fairy?" she whispered, breathless. Her heart started to pound.

Billy ducked into Tasha's room. "Yes, it's me, the Tooth Fairy," he sang as he danced around her room. She tried not to laugh. This was serious business.

"Quiet, please," she hissed. "She won't come if you're here."

"I just came to give you this." Billy dropped his phone on her bed. "You can use it as a torch. I thought it might help."

Tasha was speechless. She could hardly believe it. She didn't have a phone and she wasn't allowed the tablet upstairs. This was the nicest thing Billy had ever done. Ever.

"Thanks," she managed, totally stunned.

He shrugged his shoulders. "I didn't want you to miss it, this time." He showed her how to turn on the camera. "You could even get a selfie."

Once he'd trundled back to his room, Tasha

settled down to wait. She waited and she sat and she watched and she waited. It felt like hours. Her dim night light glowed. She could hear the TV on downstairs. In her mind, she imagined helping Billy at his tournament, but quickly stopped thinking about it, worried it would give her nightmares, not that she was falling asleep.

Gradually, her eyes began to droop. She was so tired, it would be to easy to gently drift off to sleep. She rested her head against the wall. She couldn't fall asleep. She couldn't miss the Tooth Fairy. This was her last chance to ask her wish.

"Do you think she's awake?" a voice whispered outside Tasha's door.

"Have a look."

Her head snapped up. She was so quick with Billy's phone she almost dropped it. She flicked on the torch, her heart thumping hard in her chest.

This was it. This was her moment.

Except, it wasn't the Tooth Fairy blinking in the torch light. It was Dad. He stood in the doorway with Mum close behind him.

"Why are you awake?" Dad gasped.

Mum ushered past him to tuck Tasha into bed. "Come on, now. Bedtime," she said gently.

"But... Mum, Dad," Tasha tried to complain but she was too tired. "I have... to see... the Too..."

Mum gave her a little kiss on her forehead and tiptoed out the room.

Before she knew it, the sun was already peeping in through the curtains just as she woke up.

She sat bolt upright in bed.

Oh no, she'd fallen asleep!

She couldn't believe it. Heart pounding, Tasha threw up her pillow only to find her tooth was gone.

Much to her disappointment, instead of her little, white tooth she found a shiny, golden pound coin. She pressed her lips together and breathed hard. She had missed it again! She was never going to meet a magical creature. It was hopeless. She'd have to tell Billy she couldn't help him at the tournament. She couldn't without someone granting her wish and time was running out!

Billy burst into Tasha's bedroom. "Did you see the Tooth Fairy? Did you? Did you see her?"

The look on her face told him everything.

He squeezed in beside her on her bed. "Don't worry, it's Christmas soon."

A small smile crept on Tasha's lips. Billy always had good ideas.

Chapter 3

Snowflake, the House Elf

The last autumn leaf had finally fallen leaving skinny trees swaying in the cold, winter wind. Christmas was almost here.

When Tasha thought about it, she was convinced Christmas was the best time of the year to meet magical creatures. Not only was there Father Christmas himself, she could meet elves, Mrs Claus, the reindeer, Christmas fairies, magical snowmen, talking nutcrackers, mystical ornaments, lots of things. Christmas was the most magical time of the year!

But best of all, at Christmas time, Tasha's special elf, Snowflake came to stay.

She grinned at the thought. Snowflake was a real magical creature and every Christmas she would visit Tasha and Billy. Why hadn't she thought of this to begin with? It was the perfect plan. She'd definitely be able to ask Snowflake her wish.

Snowflake was the funniest person Tasha knew. Each night in December, Snowflake would get up to special, Christmas mischief. Dad said it was his favourite part of Christmas! One time, she got all the crisp packets in the house and put them on the Christmas tree. Snowflake called it a Crisp-mas tree. So funny. Another time, Snowflake wrapped up Billy's and Tasha's school uniforms, as if they were presents *and* she ate all the chocolate from Mum's Advent calendar! Tasha had amazing Christmas adventures with her elf and she was extra excited for Snowflake to come back this year.

That morning, Snowflake had left a note explaining she'd be arriving the next day. Tasha could not wait! Not only would her elf be arriving with the Advent calendars, straight from the North Pole but Tasha would have an actual magical creature in her house. Even Billy was excited about that. He'd spent all month talking about what mischief Snowflake would get up to this year.

It was still dark when Tasha leapt out of bed and dashed downstairs to see if Snowflake had arrived.

She stood there, in the living room doorway as a huge smile spread across her face. Snowflake, Billy and Tasha's Christmas elf, dressed in red and green, was sitting on the mantelpiece as still as a statue. She was doll sized and had her same, calm smile she always had.

"Snowflake! You're back!" Tasha cried and she grabbed her elf giving her the biggest hug she'd ever given anyone. "I've missed you. I've really missed you! Listen," she said seriously, "I really need to talk to you. It's about what I put in my letter to Father Christmas. It's-"

"She's brought the Advent calendars!" Billy cried as he barged through into the living room. Tasha had barely noticed the sparkling, chocolate calendars perched on the hearth. Her wish was too important.

"Chocolate! Awesome!" Billy shouted.

Yawning and bleary eyed, Mum and Dad lurched into the living room. Their eyes were half-shut and they were still wearing their dressing gowns.

"What time is it?" asked Dad, scratching.

"Why are you so excited?" said Mum, with a yawn.

"Snowflake's back!" Billy cried. "And look!" He triumphantly held up the large, chocolate calendars with a bright, delighted grin.

Tasha smiled to herself. She had another reason to be excited about Snowflake being back. As soon as she got a chance, she was going to ask her elf the wish.

It took a few days before Tasha could be alone with Snowflake. Each time she tried, she'd spot Dad peeking through the doorway or Mum lurking nearby.

It was a Wednesday afternoon as Dad was on the loo and Mum was late at work when Tasha finally managed to talk to Snowflake alone.

She carefully took the elf off the mantelpiece and

placed her gently on the sofa. Very sensibly, she snuggled in next to her and took a deep breath, to steady her nerves.

"I hope you don't mind," said Tasha, suddenly worried she might be asking too much. "It's my wish. Well, I suppose... it's a Christmas wish now. Can you grant it?"

Snowflake didn't move. She sat there smiling straight ahead. She wasn't supposed to move of course, like those soldiers in the big, black hats outside Buckingham Palace. On holiday, Tasha had watched them for twenty whole minutes and they didn't move a muscle. Her elf was just like them. She wondered what happened when Snowflake or the soldiers had an itchy nose.

"Well, anyway," she said, getting back to the matter at hand. "This is my wish: I want to be brave like Billy. He can climb huge walls and he knows everything. He *always* has good ideas. Mum and Dad said it's just because he's older but I want to be brave, and clever too," Tasha said, thinking if she was going to ask for a wish, she'd ask for clever as a bonus, while she was at it. "Like, he knows all the cheats on games and he can climb that climbing wall, I can't do that. He can speak French and he does loads of cool things with his friends, things I can't do like climbing trees.

"Because, I don't think I'm brave enough to help Billy with his tournament." Tasha took a deep breath. "I really want to help him but it can only be done by magic. There's no other way. Can you do it?" She gently lifted Snowflake and looked into her eyes. "Can you do it? Can you make me into a better person?"

Snowflake didn't move even the tiniest bit but maybe Tasha spotted a sadness to Snowflake's eye. That couldn't be a good sign. She needed to come up with a backup plan.

It was just then that Mum arrived home. When she spotted Snowflake off the mantelpiece sitting next to Tasha, she looked serious.

"You okay, sweetie?" she asked. "What are you chatting to Snowflake about?"

"My Christmas wish," said Tasha, but she didn't smile because she wasn't sure that her elf could grant her wish.

"Oh," said Mum, "What was your wish?"

Tasha frowned as she gently placed the elf back on the mantelpiece. "I can't tell you that."

"Can you not?" asked Mum, hopefully.

"If I tell you my wish, it won't come true!"

"Of course," said Mum as Tasha skipped upstairs to play.

∞ ∞ ∞

As it turned out, after a few days, even though Tasha hadn't told anyone her wish (not even Dad or Billy, who asked three times) it didn't come true. The tournament was right after Christmas and she still wasn't brave enough to help Billy. She could barely even look at the cliff face, never mind climb it! Snowflake must have told Father Christmas her wish but maybe her elf couldn't do that sort of magic. She needed a new plan.

"Write a letter," suggested Billy. He always knew what to do. "Straight to the boss. The postal elves will come and take it to the North Pole. You could talk to them."

Her eyes lit up. "I could wear an elf costume as camouflage," she cried.

"You could…" he agreed, cautiously.

"If I dress up as an elf, they'll listen to me and take my message to Santa and I'll get my wish!"

Her brother frowned, looking doubtful. "Maybe…"

"Great!" Tasha cried. Her eyes sparkled with excitement and her heart tingled. "I'm going to ask Mum for a costume."

It took fourteen and a half asks before Mum agreed to buy the costume. Tasha had to find some ideas on the tablet and promise to wear the costume in all the family photos before Mum agreed with a sigh, "Okay, fine, I'll order it. Just, stop asking!"

The costume arrived the very next day and it was perfect. It looked exactly like Snowflake's uniform. In fact, it was identical.

"Ha!" cried Billy. "You actually look like an elf."

"She looks perfect," said Mum with a warm smile.

Tasha grinned. She'd never been so happy. Everything was going according to plan. Now all she had to do was write a letter to Father Christmas so the postal elves would arrive to collect it.

Already knowing what she wanted to write, it didn't take her long to put a letter together. She smiled, finishing her letter with, From Tasha, aged 9. She very carefully folded her letter, sticking the edges down with sparkly, Christmas stickers. She gently left it on the hearth in the living room and quietly shut the door.

"Hey, Tasha," said Billy, as she was getting into her pyjamas. "Could you check on my list, when you speak to the elves? It's the electric bike with the phone charger and the reflective panels. You won't forget, will you? I *really* want it. Like, *really*," he added with emphasis.

She promised and headed off to brush her teeth. She smiled at the costume hanging on the back of her bedroom door when she went past. It wouldn't be long now.

With a heart wrenching twist, Tasha caught a glimpse of the crossed off days on her calendar. The tournament was only a week away. If this didn't work, if she didn't get her wish, Tasha would have to tell Billy she couldn't do it.

She shook her head, no. She couldn't do that to her brother. This *had* to work.

She got into bed at bedtime, waited until everyone else had fallen asleep then crept downstairs. She quickly changed into her sparkly red and green elf costume, with white, fluffy fur around the edges. She checked the letter with the stickers was still on the fire place and settled on the sofa to wait.

It wouldn't be long now.

Chapter 4

Blitz Bookman

Tasha woke with a start to the sound of little feet scurrying around her living room. She blinked open her eyes and peeped through the blanket. There, climbing up her Christmas tree, were actual Christmas elves. She could hardly believe her eyes. Billy had been right all along, the letter had worked. She was looking at real elves. They were in her *house*.

They wore different clothes to Snowflake, Tasha's elf, but they were still dressed in shades of red and green with trimmings of white fluff.

Although, she noticed, not all the elves were quite as jolly as she'd thought they'd be. She quickly tugged the blanket over her head so none of them could see her.

"Will you two hurry up and stop messing about!" grumbled an older elf. He had wispy, white hair that poked out from under his cosy, red hat and an official looking clipboard. "This is our last house of the night. I want to get back to the North Pole so I can have my cocoa and cookies." He nudged his glasses up his nose and scratched his head with the end of his red pen. "Why they leave it this late to write the letters, I'll never know. Tomorrow is Christmas eve! Goodness me!"

"Almost got it," came a voice from Tasha's fireplace.

That was where she'd left the letter for Father Christmas, on the hearth. She risked a peep.

A grubby, rumpled looking elf mostly covered in soot was reaching for the envelope with his grubby, soot stained hands. For a moment, Tasha worried about marks on her letter. She didn't want it to look bad when Father Christmas opened it.

"Why do they make these letters so difficult to reach?" the rumpled elf complained.

"Blitz Bookman, you are asking the wrong elf," said the grumpy old elf. He wore a badge that said *Chief Noel, Head Postmaster.* "Look here, you two," he called loudly to the elves climbing the Christmas tree. "You be careful. You'll knock that tree over in a minute and then we'll all be late home."

"Check out these home made baubles!" cried one of the elves on the tree. "They're awesome. The kids worked really hard on these."

Tasha smiled to herself under the covers. She was glad the elves liked them.

"Got it!" cried Blitz Bookman, holding up the letter triumphantly. With a pang of her heart, she noticed grubby finger prints all over it.

But, she couldn't worry about that now. Tasha had to move! She had to do something. The elves had her letter and they were going to leave before she got a chance to speak to one of them. But, she wasn't as brave as Billy. He would have already burst out from his hiding place and said hello to all the elves. She wasn't like Billy.

"Wake up, lazy bones!" cried an elf climbing over the sofa. Tasha hadn't even noticed him sneaking up on her. "Can't lie down on the job, Sleepy Elf. Wake up! Wake up!" And he shook Tasha as hard as he could, rocking her out from under the blanket!

Chief Noel looked up sharply, looked at his clipboard and then glared back at Tasha.

"You're not Snowflake," he declared after some careful consideration.

Tasha shook her head, too frightened to say anything in case she got in trouble. This wasn't happening as she'd planned!

"Well, you're a House Elf, aren't you?" he demanded. "You're wearing the uniform after all. Are you lost? Is your door broken?" He pulled a face as if he didn't think much of the House Elf doors. "Well, I suppose we could give you a ride back to the North Pole, but don't go making a habit of it."

Her heart froze. A ride back to the North Pole? She could *go* to the North Pole? This wasn't what she'd planned but it was a chance she couldn't miss! It was a dream come true! No, it was better than a dream. This was real.

And, not only that, she'd be able to speak to Father Christmas himself and ask if *he* could grant her wish. She stifled a squeal of excitement.

She didn't even think about it for a second. Billy

would jump at the chance so Tasha would too. She had to be more brave, it was the only way she'd be able to help Billy with his tournament. She might as well start now.

She hopped off the sofa and followed the elves, hardly believing this was really happening. This was incredible! It was brilliant! It was the best thing that had ever happened to Tasha in all her life!

She was just about to follow the elves when Blitz, the grubby looking elf, came trundling over. He gave Tasha a quizzical look, as if he recognised her from somewhere but couldn't quite remember how he knew her. She froze hoping beyond hope that he didn't realise she was human. He shook his head at himself and trundled off after the rest of the elves.

Tasha didn't look back. This was the journey of a lifetime. As the air shimmered and twinkled around her, she found herself outside on the glittering lawn. They hadn't walked through the door, they must have walked through *magic*! A tingle of excitement fizzed in her tummy.

Little did Tasha know, this adventure was going to change her forever.

There, on the lawn in Tasha's back garden, was a sleigh. A real, North Pole sleigh. It glinted and gleamed in the moonlight and as she peered closer she spotted this sleigh had envelopes carved into the wood and golden stamps dotted here and there along the sides. Even if it wasn't Father Christmas's sleigh, it was still entirely amazing. A single, small reindeer stamped his feet at the front of the sleigh. His harness said, 'Trainee' on it. Even so, he shimmered with golden light and Tasha spotted a clever twinkle to his eye.

All the elves hopped in, leaving Tasha standing in the frosty night staring in disbelief at the sleigh. This was more than she could ever have wished for.

"We're not waiting all night," Chief Noel complained. "Come on, House Elf, get in."

Her heart bursting with excitement, Tasha climbed aboard the sleigh. Giddy and a little nervous, she fixed her eyes on the horizon as her heart filled with overwhelming delight. She was going to the North Pole!

Chapter 5

The North Pole Village

Tasha's heart beat with excitement. She was living every child's wildest dream! She was riding in a Christmas sleigh, even if it wasn't the real one and going to the North Pole. The wind streamed through her hair. The stars twinkled above her. Sparkling Christmas lights from the houses below seemed to glow and shimmer as she soared overhead. The sound of jingling sleigh bells danced through the air.

Despite shivering in the freezing cold, and her nerves rumbling in her stomach, she was grinning from ear to ear. This was something special, something magical and even if she got in trouble for it later, this was where she was meant to be.

She glided high above the vast oceans, watching continents whiz by in a joyful blur. The night twinkled with the enchantment of cities, their lights casting a magical glow that danced across the darkness. Below, rivers sparkled like shimmering ribbons of stars.

As the postal sleigh soared through the crisp, winter air, she clutched the edge of her seat, her heart pounding in her chest. In the distance, Tasha could see the magical, glimmering lights of the North Pole village. She sat up in her seat to get a better look.

Catching sight of an enormous Christmas tree, she gasped to see it twinkling in the middle of the village, towering over everything. It was bigger than a house, taller than a tower block. Every inch was covered in glittering tinsel, sparkling baubles and twinkling lights. The air around the tree crackled with golden-red light, the twinkling magic of the North Pole.

As the sleigh circled down to land, she spotted a cluster of little houses surrounding the tree with enormous warehouses and workshops dotted here and there. The sounds of joyful music filled the air, along with the sweet scent of Christmas food cooking. Her stomach rumbled. She licked her lips.

The sleigh came to rest beside the Post Office. It was unlike any building she'd ever seen before. A tall, stately construction with a bright, red roof and gleaming white walls. The outside was covered in intricate carvings of holly and ivy and the doors were decorated with golden wreaths and shiny red bows. She gazed in amazement and forgot all about hoping no one would find out she wasn't an elf. Her feet led the way.

As Tasha approached the Post Office, she felt her heart thundering with exhilaration. She couldn't believe how grand and festive the Post Office was and she couldn't wait to see what was inside.

She followed the elves lumbering past carrying the heavy post bags as she tried to look at everything at once!

She could barely believe her eyes as she slipped through the great doors and into the Post Office. She was greeted by the sight of a vast, airy room filled with rows upon rows of shelves and cubbies. Busy sounds stuffed the air with commotion and voices. Hundreds of elves rushed everywhere with stacks of letters and packages, their bright red and green outfits a blur of colour.

She gasped in wonder, desperate to explore and see every part of the North Pole magic!

She shook her head, coming to her senses. Tasha had a mission. She didn't have time to explore. She had to find Father Christmas and ask her wish, and become a better person, like her brother. Only then, could she help Billy with his tournament.

"Come on then, House Elf," said Chief Noel. "Better make yourself useful."

He waved his hand above his head and suddenly envelopes began shooting towards Tasha's face. She ducked and looked up to find five envelopes slotted neatly into Chief Noel's hand. He handed them to her.

"You don't say much, do you?" Chief Noel observed, with a lift of his eyebrow.

Tasha stayed quiet. She was too worried he'd notice she was just a girl and not an elf at all. She didn't want to know what would happen if he found out, but she was sure it would have something to do with the Naughty List.

"These letters need to go directly to the toy workshop," said Chief Noel. "Be quick about it, before they lose their magic."

She nodded and hurried out the door. She did look back, catching a quick glance over her shoulder. The Post Office was incredible.

Just as she pulled the door shut, a cloud of envelopes whooshed around the Post Office in a erratic frenzy and stopped. The cloud suddenly dropped like a bucket of papery water all over Chief Noel's head.

"Hmm," said Chief Noel thoughtfully, emerging from under the mound of envelopes. "That's not happened before. I wonder..." He cast a thoughtful gaze at the door Tasha had walked through.

Chapter 6

The Nutcrackers

Nothing Tasha had ever seen in her entire life, nor that she would see since, had ever been as amazing as what was on the other side of the Post Office door. She stood frozen in amazement, forgetting all about the letters Chief Noel had stuffed into her pocket.

Before her stretched the North Pole village. It lay under a blanket of soft, fluffy snow from the roofs of the beautiful, little elf houses to the bushes and snow-capped trees. Warm, cheerful lights were strung up between the buildings and curled around twinkling trees. Jolly music drifted through the air along with the delicious smell of cookies baking. Her tummy rumbled.

The delightful hustle and bustle of a busy Christmas village wasn't too far away and it all merged with the noise from the hectic sorting office.

The strangest part of it all was, she didn't feel cold at all. Despite the snow and the night sky, the North Pole Village felt warm and cosy.

"Oh! Perfect! A House Elf," a twinkling voice cried from the path in front of her. "We need to ask you a question."

With her heart in her mouth, trying to appear as elf-like as possible, Tasha looked over to see a Christmas fairy. She was fluttering in the air beside a snowman who lifted his black top hat and gave her a friendly nod. She could barely believe this was really happening.

"Hello," Tasha managed to squeak, utterly stunned. She staggered towards them, her legs so shocked by a friendly nod from a snowman that they forgot how to work. The fairy and the snowman gave her a quizzical look but much to Tasha's relief, they didn't say anything about it.

"You go into lots of houses," the fairy began in her light, tinkling voice. "What goes on the top of the Christmas Tree? A fairy…"

"Or a star?" the snowman interrupted. "It's a star, isn't it?"

Tasha didn't know what to say. She had a seen all sorts of wonderful things on the top of Christmas trees at her friends' houses. Then she remembered one particular tree she'd seen in a Christmas shop.

"Some… some," Tasha stuttered. She was talking to a real Christmas fairy and a real snowman after all. She cleared her throat. "Uh, some Christmas trees have feathers sprouting out the top."

Both the snowman and the fairy had a good giggle at the sound of that. Tasha beamed.

"What will they think of next?" the fairy asked between giggles. She shook her head in disbelief.

"Lovely to meet you," said the snowman

pleasantly.

"I.. yes... I..." Tasha stammered.

She couldn't believe it. A snowman and a Christmas fairy! As the snowman and fairy headed off down the snow lined path, Tasha made her way into the village. She didn't see, but the snowman's carrot nose fell clean off his face and tumbled down to the snow. Luckily, his fairy friend quickly swooped down and pushed the carrot back into place.

"That's never happened before," the snowman complained, but he thanked the fairy for her help even so.

All around Tasha, the air sparkled with excitement. It was the night before Christmas Eve and the whole of the North Pole was busy getting ready. Final preparations were well underway and finishing touches were added to special toys.

Everywhere she looked, warm light shone from the windows and the sounds of happy merriment floated through each open doorway.

She found her feet were leading her towards the enormous Christmas tree at the centre of the village. Up close, it was even more colossal than she'd thought, wider than her house. It made her dizzy just looking up at it.

Easily distracted, the sound of complaining caught Tasha's attention. She followed the sound into a square between the houses and, to her amazement, discovered an entire company of nutcrackers. She gazed in astonishment at their shiny uniforms, their straight backs and fancy hats. Each one looked like an child-sized version of the nutcrackers Billy had in his room!

There was just one problem: they all looked miserable. Instead of marching about, they were standing around, forlorn and lost.

"What's the matter?" she asked the nearest nutcracker, forgetting all about trying to hide that she wasn't really an elf.

"We don't have a drummer," he complained. "We march all out of sync without a drummer."

"Oh, no. That's sad," Tasha agreed. She was about to leave when the nutcracker perked up as if he'd had an idea.

"Hey, I don't suppose you could be our drummer, could you?" he asked hopefully.

Tasha quickly shook her head. "No, I wouldn't be any good."

"How will you know if you don't try?" the nutcracker told her. "Here, lads!" he called to the company of nutcrackers, "I've found us a drummer."

"No! Wait!" But it was too late.

A cheer rose up from the nutcrackers and they quickly got into formation in the middle of the square. They looked very smart indeed but Tasha couldn't be their drummer. She had no idea what she was doing. They'd all look at her when she got it wrong, and she'd upset everyone.

"Here's the drum," said the nutcracker, not noticing her worried expression. "And the sticks. You'll be great! Hit them like this."

And he quickly showed her how to hit the drum.

She tired to explain to the nutcrackers again, "I don't think I'd be very –"

"Thank you so much!" the nutcracker cried. "We'd never be able to practice without you."

He hurried off to his place in the company and gave Tasha a reassuring grin. She didn't feel reassured. She felt hopeless.

With no way to escape without drawing attention to herself, she took a deep breath and hit the drum gently. Nothing happened until one of the nutcrackers called over asking her to play a little louder.

With her nerves bubbling in her stomach, Tasha hit the drum again and again. She was terrified of making a mistake in front of everyone so it was a wobbly start. Before long, she started to grin as her drumming gradually got better and better. Her chest swelled with pride as she realised she was part of a team.

The nutcrackers marched around the square in perfect formation, thanks to the help of Tasha's drumming. They looked amazing, all of them turning with a simultaneous snap and their boots hitting the cobble stones at the exact same moment. She was so impressed that as soon as they were done, she dropped the drumsticks and gave them all an enthusiastic round of applause.

"You're pretty good with the drums," said the nutcracker. "Do you think you might like to join our company?"

"We'd love to have you!" cried another nutcracker.

"You're the best drummer we've ever had," said another.

It was a tempting offer. Tasha had never been so proud of herself.

"Thank you .. but.." She remembered the letters in her pocket but most importantly, the reason why she was at the North Pole in the first place. She was here to see Father Christmas and ask him to grant her Christmas wish. She couldn't get distracted now. Billy's tournament was at stake. "I'm sorry but I have a lot to do," she told them politely.

And with that, she left the drum and the sticks and went off to find Father Christmas's house.

She didn't notice but as she walked away, one of the nutcracker's arms fell off with a clatter to the ground. He was quickly repaired by his kind, nutcracker friends but he couldn't help but wonder.

"That's not happened before," he said thoughtfully.

Chapter 7

The Candy Kitchen

The North Pole village was a lot trickier to get around than Tasha had first thought. She was no closer to finding Father Christmas's house than she was when she left the Post Office!

As she wandered through the North Pole Village, she was amazed by all the incredible sights. Led by her nose, it wasn't long before she found her way to the candy kitchen. Her tummy rumbled. It quickly made the decision to head inside.

Her mouth watered as she slipped through the doorway.

She was immediately hit with warmth and the sweet smell of deliciousness. She gulped in sugary scents as she made her way through the busy kitchen, following her nose. The sounds of bubbling pots and clanging spoons, delightful kitchen sounds filled the air.

Bright colours shone from every shelf and table. Endless rows of sweetie jars lined the walls piled high on shelves, filling the room with vibrant, cheerful colours of every shade. Busy elves wearing splattered aprons rushed about while pots stirred themselves and mixtures poured from bowls. She was amazed. Elves were busy chopping and whisking, stretching and looping and best of all, some of the elves were taste testing. She headed that way.

But before she could taste any sweets, she noticed a plump little elf with half rimmed glasses perched on the end of her nose fretting over her bubbling pot. She didn't look jolly at all.

"Oh deary me, I don't know what's going wrong. Oh, what a to do," the elf moaned. "It's red but it's supposed to be purple. I followed the recipe exactly! Oh dear, oh dear."

Tasha liked her immediately. She looked just like Dad when he was puzzling over his cooking, with her glasses perched right on the end of her nose like that. Tasha was determined to see what she could do to help. Taste testing would have to wait.

She peeped into the enormous cooking pot and the mixture was indeed a bright, Christmassy shade of red. The smells billowing in the steam from the pot made her stomach rumble again. She took a long, scrumptious sniff and smiled to herself.

"What am I going to do, dear?" the elf wailed. "It was clear in the letter, the little boy wanted *purple* sweets. I'm going to ruin Christmas!"

Tasha bit her lip and rubbed the elf's arm reassuringly. She wasn't sure what to say, the elf looked so worried and upset. Tasha wanted to help but she had no idea where to start. Billy would have known what to do.

She thought for a moment, looking at the jars lined up on the table beside the cooking pot. She stood up on her tiptoes and peeped once more into the pot.

"Red and blue make purple," she explained, "Could you add some of this blue colouring to the pot to make the red turn purple?"

The elf paused. She looked at the jar of blue colouring. Then, she looked into the pot. She picked up the blue colouring and inspected it closely. Tasha's heart began to pound as she wondered if she'd said something wrong.

Suddenly, the elf beamed a bright smile. "What a fabulous idea!" she cried. "My dear, you are brilliant! I would never have thought of that. Thank you."

The elf grabbed Tasha and gave her the biggest, warmest, jolliest hug she'd ever had. She smiled back shyly. Her chest puffed out a little as she felt proud of herself for helping someone. This was turning out to be one of the best nights of Tasha's entire life.

She even managed to find her way to the taste testing area and gobbled down far too many sweets for that late at night. Her mum would have a lot to say about that, if she'd been there, but as mum wasn't, Tasha pocketed a few more sweets to eat later. Her pockets bulged.

Before she made her way out the sweet factory, she had an idea.

"Excuse me," she said to the plump elf she'd helped who was now happily stirring a purple mixture in her cooking pot. "Could you tell me how to get to Father Christmas's house?"

The elf looked at her puzzled. "Have you forgotten, dear?" she asked. "It's where it always is."

Tasha froze, trying to think of an excuse. "I.. er... I'm.." she remembered Mum's words. "I'm just a bit muddle headed today."

The elf gave Tasha a sympathetic smile. "We all have those days, dear." She wiped her hands on her apron and turned to face Tasha. "Right. You go through the bubble room, past the stock cupboard. When you see the reindeer barn, you'll spot the sleigh shed on your left. After that, Father Christmas's house is right next to the toy workshop. Did you get that, dear?"

She nodded, thinking she could just about remember it all and turned to leave. Just as Tasha headed out the door, she noticed Chief Noel walking in through the back. He was still carrying his clipboard. He stood out in his pristine postal elf uniform as everyone else in the sweet factory wore splattered aprons. He spoke to the plump elf she'd helped while she hid around a corner to listen.

"I'm looking for a house elf," he said, "Have you seen one?"

"Oh yes, dear," said the plump elf, "She was around here somewhere. Oh - but she seems to have gone now."

"Hmm," said Chief Noel, sounding disappointed. "Something tricky is going on around here."

Her heart pounding, Tasha dashed out the sweet

factory door and quickly made her way down the snow lined path. Now, she had to avoid Snowflake, her house elf, *and* Chief Noel if she was ever going to find Father Christmas and ask her Christmas wish in time. This was not good at all! Especially if Chief Noel was on her trail.

Suddenly, back in the candy kitchen, vats and pots began to pop and burst, spewing their sugary – and above all - *sticky* mixture into the air.

"Oh dear!" exclaimed the elves as goo rained down all around them.

"Look out!"

A huge dollop of gloopy, pink mixture splattered onto Chief Noel's head, dripping down his face with a splat onto his official looking clipboard.

"Oh dear," said the kind, plump elf with her hands on her hips. "That's never happened before."

Chapter 8

The Tinsel Forest

Lost in thought and not at all watching where she was going, Tasha found herself strolling through a forest that was like no other.

Starlight flittered through the branches reflecting from shiny tinsel creating a dazzling display.

Instead of leaves, each tree branch was adorned with long strands of tinsel that shimmered and sparkled in every colour under the bright moonlight. She could hear the gentle rustling of tinsel in the breeze.

"I'm in a tinsel forest!" Tasha gasped.

The North Pole really was a place of wonder, where *anything* was possible.

"Oh, I'll never be done in time," muttered a voice from somewhere beneath the swishing tinsel. "Never be done in time. This is terrible."

"Hello?" Tasha called out.

With a rustle of tinsel and a stomp of his feet, a small, gnarled elf erupted through the trees. He wore rumpled forest greens with only the tiniest hint of red on his bobble hat which wobbled merrily.

"A house elf? A house elf?" He peered at her in the costume that looked exactly like Snowflake's uniform. "I don't have time for this!" and he started to bustle off back into the trees, taking his bad temper with him.

"Wait!" Tasha called, "Are you alright?"

"Alright? Alright?" he grumbled. "She asks if I'm alright. Well, no I'm not." He shook his head.

He certainly is not a jolly, old elf, she thought to herself. Part of her wished she hadn't walked into the forest at all but now she was here, she wanted to help. She listened carefully.

"It's almost Christmas Eve – almost Christmas Eve! - and my team are busy helping in the toy workshop – the toy workshop!" he griped. "I've got no one – no one - to help me harvest the tinsel. What will Father Christmas think if he's got no tinsel in his house. In his house! He's Father Christmas! Father Christmas!"

"You're taking the tinsel to Father Christmas's house?" Tasha asked eagerly. This could be her chance, her one moment to go straight to Father Christmas's house. While she was excited to see the rest of the North Pole village, she knew it wouldn't be long before Chief Noel caught up with her. She wanted to ask her Christmas wish before it was too late.

"Well? Well? Where else!"

"I can help you."

He peered at her suspiciously. "A house elf? A

house elf? Hmm." He sighed. "I'll take all the help I can get!"

She set to work, carefully pulling strings of soft, glimmering tinsel from the branches around her. She wondered what Billy would make of all this.

It turned out, Father Christmas liked sparkling brown and forest green tinsel in his house so that's just what Tasha helped the elf, who's name was Marley, pick from the trees. In no time at all, they had filled three, large baskets with beautiful, shimmering tinsel.

With his hands on his hips, Marley regarded the baskets with a satisfied grin. "Done a good job there, a good job. Yes."

Tasha beamed with pride. She was getting the hang of being helpful.

"Right, I'd better get these off to Father Christmas's house. To Father Christmas's house, you see."

Tasha rushed to pick up one of the baskets to help Marley carry them, but he hoisted one onto his back and the other two he wore across his shoulders.

She bit her lip and asked, "Wouldn't you like me to help you take them?"

"Balanced now, see? Balanced," he explained, showing Tasha how the baskets rested on his shoulders. "Thanks for all your help. Thanks. Might need to make you a forest elf, instead."

"But.. I…" She *had* to go with Marley!

She raced after him, dashing through the trees. Branch after branch smacked her on the nose, or tangled through her legs trying to trip her up. She lost sight of Marley! All she could hear was his cheerful humming somewhere off in the distance.

If she couldn't follow Marley, how was she going to get to Father Christmas's house? She'd already forgotten all of the cooking elf's directions, except for one: the reindeer barn.

That's where she'd head to next.

As Tasha made her way back into the village, one strand of tinsel drifted loose from its branch and landed in complete silence on the snow. In its place unfurled a perfect, green leaf.

Marley paused what he was doing and peered closely at the leaf.

"Hmm," he hmmed, thoughtfully, "That's never happened before."

Chapter 9

The North Pole Weather Station

Tasha crept through the North Pole village, grinning up at the hanging lights and the sparkling snow draped over all the buildings. She was on her way to find the reindeer barn, and after that, Father Christmas's house where she could ask her Christmas wish.

She kept her eyes peeled for Snowflake and Chief Noel, hoping she wouldn't bump into them just yet. At least, not until she met Father Christmas.

She eyed the towering Christmas tree which rose over everything. She did smile at it, because even though the tree was dizzyingly tall, it was festively beautiful. The golden star twinkled at the top of the tree, beaming with light and magic over the village. She shuddered at the thought of climbing a tree this big to put the star at the top. She didn't envy whoever had to do that!

Unfortunately, lost in her thoughts, Tasha had forgotten all about avoiding Snowflake, the elf who visited her house, who would know Tasha was a human girl and not an elf at all. She was certain, her house elf would definitely send Tasha back to the human world.

Snowflake was exactly the person who came walking around the very next corner, with a whole group of house elves.

Tasha froze. It would be only seconds before Snowflake saw her. She had to run, she had to hide! She had to go in the opposite direction but it was too late.

Luckily, Snowflake was chatting to the other house elves and hadn't seen Tasha yet.

She dipped into the shadows under a drooping roof, hoping that would be enough but Snowflake was heading straight towards her!

She rushed back to the building. As she thumped her back hard against the wall, a dollop of snow tumbled from the roof and covered Tasha just as Snowflake walked past with her group of house elves.

Tasha held her breath.

She was covered in snow from head to toe. No one could tell who was standing there. Only her eyes peeped through. She looked like a friendly snow person.

The house elves were so close Tasha could hear them talking. They couldn't see her. No one could, under all that snow.

"Her wish was so sad," said Snowflake to her friends, "I wanted to help her see how amazing she is all by herself."

Tasha wondered who her elf could be talking

about. Could she mean Billy?

She was too nervous to worry about that now. She *couldn't* get spotted by Snowflake. She *couldn't* be sent home. She imagined Billy's face when she told him she couldn't help him in the tournament. That was the whole reason she'd come to the North Pole in the first place: to ask her wish and be braver. She *couldn't* be spotted.

Her heart was thumping so loudly she was sure Snowflake would hear it.

Instead, the elf carried on chatting to her friends as they walked on by.

Tasha breathed a sigh of relief. She had done it!

Unfortunately, when the last elf walked past her, she gave the Tasha-shaped snow person a second look. The elf was pretty, with curly black hair, a warm smile and a suspicious glare.

"Has someone been making new snow people?" the elf called to her friends.

The group of house elves stopped and turned back to look. Tasha's heart started to pound again. She held her breath even though her chest was bursting. She couldn't move. She tried not to blink!

"Aw, that's a good one," said Snowflake. "I wonder who made it."

"It needs a scarf," said one of Snowflake's friends, and she took off the scarf she was wearing to wrap it around Tasha's snow covered neck. She tried not to move.

"Much better," Snowflake agreed, as the group of house elves walked on.

Tasha didn't move for at least five more minutes, not until she was absolutely sure the house elves were completely gone. When she couldn't see them or even hear them at all, she shook off the snow and hurried away in the opposite direction.

That was too close, Tasha thought to herself. She had to be much more careful and watch where she was going. If it hadn't been for the snow, Tasha would be headed back to the human world right now. She'd had a lucky escape but she had to think more carefully next time.

That was when she spotted some elves wearing green and red overalls. On their backs they had, large bails of hay and carried dirty shovels. They must be elves who looked after the reindeer! Tasha grinned to herself. She had to be close to Father Christmas's house by now!

As she got closer to the reindeer elves, Tasha noticed giant baubles soaring above her head. They were on a cable, as if they were cable cars, and elves were hopping in and out of them as they landed in the square. The baubles were all colours and each one shimmered and shined. They all had doors and windows cut into them.

"Hey! You there!" called Chief Noel from the other side of the square. "House elf!"

He'd found her! Tasha couldn't believe it! She should have been paying more attention! To Tasha's horror, Chief Noel was heading in her direction.

She glanced back at the reindeer elves, achingly close to Father Christmas's house, reluctantly hopped onto one of the passing baubles and was quickly scooped up into the air away from Chief Noel. He stood glaring up at her as she soared out of reach.

The bauble lifted Tasha up and over the North Pole village, almost as high as the star at the top of the Christmas Tree. She soared over the houses onto a little hill just outside the village. She was the only one to get off here, but it seemed well enough away from Chief Noel to be safe.

Unfortunately, it was also very far from Father Christmas's house.

She hopped off the bauble into a vast empty hallway. This seemed like a good place to hide from Chief Noel. As the bauble trundled away, Tasha wandered on, to see what she could find.

"Hello?" Tasha called out into the echoey hallway. "Hello!"

Round a draughty corridor, she discovered a huge, glinting sphere, surrounded by golden rings that span in all sorts of directions. Her mouth dropped open in amazement.

"What is it?" she gasped to herself.

"Chairs are over there," said a voice behind her, making her jump.

She span around to see a wizened old elf leaning on a gnarled walking stick shuffling towards her. He had jolly red cheeks with a warm smile and wore a crumpled old suit of red and green.

"Hello," she said, "What is this statue?"

"I can show you where the toilets are," the wise

old elf said, blushing a little.

She frowned, wondering why he said that. Then.. suddenly, she realised! "I don't want a poo!" she cried. "The statue! Statue! What's it for?"

Standing beside her, the elf shook his wise, old head. "Shut the door?" he asked, confused. He soon rallied and said, "I bet you're wondering about this statue." He pointed his walking stick at the swirling sphere with the golden rings. "This is the North Pole Weather Station," he told her proudly. "We don't get many house elves up here. I'm glad you're taking an interest. This is where we make sure the weather is safe for Father Christmas's special delivery night."

"Wow," Tasha gasped, gazing up at the enormous, magical sculpture. "The North Pole Weather Station." She watched the rings sliding around the sphere as the light glinted on the metal. "Thank you," she said with a smile.

"Come on, the toilets are this way," said the elf, starting to shuffle off to the way he'd come.

"No! No!" she cried, "I'm okay! I'll go now. Good bye."

"Oh yes, please, bring me back some pie."

She giggled to herself as she made her way back out of the Weather Station and towards the bauble cable car. She thought she'd better get a move on before Chief Noel discovered where she was. From her spot on the hill, Tasha could see the entire village shining warmly beneath the enormous Christmas tree.

But the warmest, jolliest and brightest home of

them all sat next to the reindeer barn and opposite the sleigh shed. The biggest smile she'd ever smiled grew on her lips as excitement fizzed in her tummy. It was Father Christmas's house! Now, all she had to do was get there.

Just in that moment, Tasha remembered the letters still in her pocket. The toy workshop was the largest building in the entire village, and it was next to the reindeer barn, just like the cooking elf had told her. She formed a cunning plan. First, she'd drop off the letters and then, she'd be able to find Father Christmas and ask her wish.

As she stepped onto the bauble cable car, she heard a clang echo through the North Pole weather station. She didn't give it any further thought but the old elf scratched his head in confuddlement as he picked up the cog that had fizzed out of the machine.

"How strange," he said to himself. "That's not happened before."

Chapter 10

The Toy Workshop

Now that Tasha knew where she was going, she felt a lot more confident. She strode through the village, smiling and saying hello to flittering fairies, grinning gingerbread men and thumping snowmen all at the same time as keeping her eyes peeled for Chief Noel and Snowflake the elf.

The nutcrackers tipped their hats at her as she went past and groups of elves called a friendly hello. She felt right at home.

When she arrived outside the North Pole Toy Workshop, her mouth dropped open. She stopped and stared. The building was enormous and all the sounds coming from inside set the ground shaking beneath her feet. She licked her lips, took a deep breath and pushed open the huge, toy workshop doors, that were just as heavy as they looked.

The sight took her breath away. Hundreds, or maybe even thousands of elves were working on every imaginable toy. The workshop seemed to stretch on endlessly, with conveyor belts whirring and pipes snaking along the walls, carrying materials and magic to the bustling workstations.

Tasha gazed around in wonder.

The inside of the factory was even more enormous than the outside. Four levels looped the workshop packed with elves all busily working away. The sound of humming came from an elf nearby, his nimble fingers sewing together a beautiful doll with love and care. Two cheerful elves worked side by side, joyfully putting a toy train together, their laughter filling the air. Conveyor belts hummed and whirred, transporting partially completed toys to different stations, where the skilled elves added their magical touches. Pipes twisted and turned overhead, carrying magical materials that fuelled the making of each special toy.

Through it all, the magic of Christmas danced in the air. She could sense the love and care that went into every stitch, every brushstroke, and every twist of wire. The workshop was a place where dreams became real, where imagination exploded, and where the magic of toys came to life.

As the elves put the finishing touches on their toys, she couldn't help but feel the excitement building. That night, on Christmas Eve, the toys would be ready to bring smiles and laughter to children all over the world – and she was one of them!

Suddenly, excitement gripped her heart. She almost squealed in delight as she caught sight of Father Christmas at the back of the workshop. There he was, working on creating a very special toy using his own, glittering tools. His face was creased, deep in concentration as his hands worked deftly on the toy. Tasha couldn't help but wonder who it was for.

As if hypnotised, unable to look anywhere but at Father Christmas himself, she pulled the letters out her pocket and absently passed them to the nearest elf without a word.

She stepped through the workshop as if in a trance, slipping between tables, stepping over boxes and dodging around rushing elves as she made her way towards Father Christmas.

Her heart was pounding. She practiced what she was going to say in her head. She needed this wish to help Billy in his tournament. Father Christmas would understand that. He was right there, so close she could almost touch him.

Her throat went dry. This was finally going to happen. She almost couldn't believe it. She was about to speak to Father Christmas, the most magical person in the entire world. If anyone could grant Tasha's wish, it would be Father Christmas.

"A house elf?" came a voice to the side of her, "Are you lost? You must be new."

She wasn't listening. "Yeah," she replied absentmindedly.

"A new elf!" cried the voice. "Everyone! A new elf!"

"A new elf?" shouted another voice.

"A new elf!"

Tasha looked around in surprise. What had she walked into? She was going to get caught at the

North Pole! A human dressed as an elf, they were going to send her home. She couldn't believe it, she was so close! This was the worst timing! Why couldn't the elves leave her alone? She needed to speak to Father Christmas!

She backed away, holding up her hands, searching for an escape.

Father Christmas looked up from the toy he was making, frowning with confusion at all the shouting.

"Hurrah!" the elves cheered. They dropped their tools and headed in Tasha's direction. All of them! The elves on the upper floors leaned over the railings to get a better look.

"Yay! A new elf!"

"A new friend!"

"We should celebrate!"

That got a resounding cheer! The crowd of elves poured out the workshop. She could do nothing but get swept along with them, away from Father Christmas who was watching them with a very confused look on his face.

Tasha was jostled and pressed forward, as elves patted her on the back and led her away from the workshop, through the North Pole village.

Father Christmas was on his feet, scratching his head.

"I didn't request a new elf," he said to someone. It could have been Chief Noel.

Tasha tried to look over the little elf heads to see where she was going in the hope that she could find her way back but they turned her around and were so pleased to see her that she couldn't tell the way.

She didn't notice, but on Father Christmas's work table, the head of the little doll he was making popped off and rolled under the table.

"How curious," he said. "That's never happened before."

It wasn't until the crowd of elves arrived at a very warm, very jolly building that they stopped and let Tasha get her bearings. Jolly, singing voices came from inside and the toy workshop elves piled in, taking Tasha inside with them. She soon found herself in a jolly canteen filled with elves, nutcrackers, snow-people, fairies, gingerbread people and many more magical creatures besides. Everywhere she looked, she spotted them all sipping on steaming hot chocolate and munching on chocolate chip cookies.

"Welcome to the North Pole!" one of the toy workshop elves called brightly as he handed Tasha a large mug of steaming hot chocolate.

She held the mug carefully in her hands and deeply breathed in the steam. Never, in Tasha's entire life had she ever smelt anything so delicious, not even in the candy kitchen. If the excitement of Christmas and presents and snowball fights and decorations could be boiled up into one, delicious smell, this was what the hot chocolate smelt like.

"Drink up!" cried the elves, with chocolate moustaches on their top lips and cream on the point of their noses. Tasha giggled.

She took a tiny sip and instantly magic swirled across her tongue. The hot chocolate was the perfect temperature. It was the optimum mixture of chocolate and milk, not too chocolatey, not too milky. Taste and tingles burst in her mouth as she gulped down the most delectable hot chocolate in the entire world! Her tummy warmed.

"That's amazing!" Tasha cried. "That's the best hot chocolate I've ever had!"

The elves cheered and there was more slapping her on the back as they grinned at her and hurrahed. They all thought she was one of them. This was the best day of Tasha's life!

"So, New Elf," said one of the toy workshop elves, the oldest and jolliest looking of them all, "What is your name?"

"Natasha," said Tasha, "But everyone calls me Tasha."

The toy workshop elf nodded in approval. "A good, strong Christmas name," he declared, much to the cheering of the other elves. "And your birthday is Christmas Day? We will be able to celebrate the day after tomorrow! We must prepare a party!"

Tasha frowned, feeling confused. "No.. my birthday is in Ju-"

"Cousin!" cried an elf from the crowd. Tasha's eyes widened in shock and dismay as she spotted the rumpled, sooty elf from her house charging his way through the crowd. "Cousin, how great to see you again." He threw an arm across Tasha's shoulders. "She gets confused, her birthday most definitely is the day after tomorrow: Christmas Day! Hurrah!"

The other elves cheered, "Hurrah!"

"What are you doing?" Tasha hissed.

"Play along," the elf hissed back. Tasha remembered his name was Blitz. "Play along and we might just get out of this without anyone finding out."

He knew! He *knew* she wasn't an elf. This was the elf who'd kept looking at her strangely in the postal sleigh. Her heart sank. She'd been worried about Chief Noel and Snowflake all this time, but it was the postal elves she should have watched out for.

She hoped she'd be able to sneak away and see Father Christmas before Blitz told on her.

"Come with me," Blitz muttered as he shimmied through the crowds and out into the cool North Pole air.

Tasha trudged through the crowd behind him, dreading what he was going to say. This was awful. It was what she'd been worrying about. Tasha had been caught.

"Are you going to tell on me?" she asked glumly when she finally arrived outside.

"Go home!" Blitz snapped. He was not jolly at all. "Just, go home. You shouldn't be here. You're going to ruin everything."

"I… I…" Tasha didn't know what to say. "I won't," she whispered.

"It's probably already too late." Blitz shook his head. "Just go."

"But wait, I need to speak to Father Christmas,

first. I have…I have this.. Well, this Christmas wish. But it's not really for me, it's for my brother."

Blitz raised his eyebrows, held up his hands and took a few steps back from Tasha shaking his head. "Oh no, no way. No. No way. Absolutely not. No. No! Definitely not! No. No!"

"But, I'm lost," she pleaded.

"I'm already in trouble about the List, there's no way I am going to help," he angrily whispered the next part, "a human child!" He shook his head. "I'll get in even more trouble. He'll have me working in the reindeer sheds next. No way, Tasha, you're on your own. Sorry."

She gasped. "How do you know my name?"

"Really? After you announced it to the entire North Pole?"

"But, but you knew me before that," she said, remembering how Blitz had looked at her in her living room. "You knew I wasn't an elf."

"Well.. I…," Blitz shuffled his feet and looked down. "I used to work on the List. You get to know all the kids that way."

"Wait.. what's wrong with the List?" she asked, hoping her name wasn't on the naughty list. "Why are you in trouble about the List?"

She pulled her new elf scarf around her neck. It was getting chilly. She hoped beyond hope that the List wasn't broken and most importantly, her name was on the Nice List.

"Nothing now, and they've repaired the roof. Apparently, you can't even tell there was an explosion."

"You blew up the Naughty and Nice List?" Tasha gasped. She was really beginning to worry which List her name was on, now.

"Not the whole thing, and not on purpose," Blitz told her, grumpily. "But that doesn't change anything. You've *got to go*!"

But where, Tasha wondered, and how?

Chapter 11

The Naughty and Nice List

After Blitz had stomped off in a huff, leaving Tasha alone once more in the middle of the North Pole Village, she decided her best way home was to find Father Christmas and ask him to grant her wish.

Still, she couldn't help wondering what had made Blitz so cross and why he'd wanted her to leave the North Pole so quickly. She hadn't done anything wrong, had she?

It was just as she was wondering and wandering through the North Pole village, lost in her own thoughts, that she heard three very important words.

"Ho! Ho! Ho!"

She froze, her eyes wide. Her heart was pounding, she almost couldn't believe her ears. There he was, right in front of her: Father Christmas himself. This was her chance! Finally, she could ask her Christmas wish. Nothing could distract her now. No one was trying to drag her away.

She took a deep breath but just as she was about to head over to Father Christmas, she heard two more words. Unfortunately, these words made her stop in her tracks.

"Hello, Snowflake!" said Father Christmas cheerfully.

The one elf in the whole of the North Pole who could have spotted Tasha was human girl and not an elf at all was walking straight towards her. This was getting too close!

As disappointment hung heavy in her heart and frustration boiled in her mind, she knew she'd have to try again later. She couldn't let her house elf see her her, not here. She'd be sent home before her wish even passed her lips! She hurried away, keeping her head down.

Unfortunately, that meant she wasn't looking where she was going and walked straight into the path of Chief Noel, who was coming the other way. Tasha froze. She didn't know what to do, or which way to go. Nothing was going to plan! This was a disaster.

"Ah, I've been looking for you," said Chief Noel, pulling out his magical, festive clipboard.

She didn't wait to find out what he wanted. Instead, she ducked through the nearest doorway, ignoring the sign saying 'authorised personnel only.'

She was surprised to find she was in a grand room filled from floor to ceiling with more books than she had ever seen in her life. The walls were lined with stuffed bookcases and pages lay scattered around the floor or poking out from books here and there on the shelves.

Elves were hard at work in here too and all of them were sat quietly reading. If they weren't pouring over a piece of paper, they were flicking through the pages of books or searching the shelves. A hushed silence hung in the air. After the bustling noise of the toy workshop, she was grateful to pause in the quiet stillness. No one paid any attention to her and she wondered if that could be because *she* wasn't a book.

A lectern, a small, glinting pillar of wood, stood alone in the centre of the room. She was immediately drawn to it. It's magical glow glittered into the dusty gloom of the room.

At the top of the lectern sat the most enormous book she had ever seen. It was wide open and through the middle of it lay a beautiful, satin ribbon bookmark.

In front of the lectern, she stood on a small box that brought her up to the perfect height to read the book.

She gasped. Her eyes widened. She couldn't believe what she'd found.

"It's The List!" she whispered.

She poured over the book, carefully reading the names. The List was one place she'd always wondered about and was glad she'd stumbled onto it. Plus, she was even more curious now that Blitz said he blew it up! She couldn't spot any sign of an explosion, though, thankfully.

On one side of the book, names appeared in a scrolling list with golden sparkles glittering on the page like written stars. On the other side, green ink wrote names slowly.

"The Nice List," she said, looking at the golden writing, "and the Naughty List," she whispered eying the green ink.

Blazing bright on the page in glittering, gold writing was Billy's name. Tasha grinned. Of course, her brother was on the Nice List. She wondered where her name could be. She bit her lip, feeling anxiety building in the pit of her stomach. Could she really be on the Naughty List?

She jumped as she spotted a name she recognised written in green ink. She couldn't believe it and blinked twice after rubbing her eyes just to be sure.

"Hmm, makes sense," she said to herself.

It was with great relief that Tasha finally spotted her own name written in golden ink sparkling away on the Nice List. She felt a wave of relief wash over her. She was unbelievably grateful that Father Christmas knew how good she'd been all year. She'd even tidied her room without being asked, once, in April but it still counted.

Just as she hopped down from the lectern, she caught sight of her golden name flickering. None of the other names flickered. She leapt up onto the box only to see her name blaze and disappear from the Nice List completely.

She gasped, her hands over her mouth. Searching the page, her eyes wide with panic, a sick feeling filled her tummy.

"Where did it go?" she whispered franticly,

scanning the page for a sign, anything, some trace of her name.

Much to her dismay, her name started flickering and blinking again but this time in green ink on the Naughty List.

"What?" she gasped.

Her tummy somersaulted. She couldn't believe this was happening. Tasha couldn't be on the Naughty List, she just couldn't! This was impossible. She was good, well behaved! Mum always said so.

Just as she was about to lose all hope, her name disappeared from the Naughty List and reappeared once again in glittering gold writing on the Nice List. She felt a wave of relief until her name flickered once more and reappeared yet again in green ink on the Naughty List.

"What's going on?" she asked herself, puzzled.

"Are you supposed to be in here?" snapped an elf from behind Tasha, making her yelp in alarm.

She span and stepped down from the box. "I... er... well," she began, still whirling from seeing her name on the Naughty List. She couldn't think straight. Why was her name flickering? Had she been naughty? Her mind whirled in a fog of confusion.

"A house elf!" the List Elf exclaimed, upon seeing Tasha's costume, "I should have known. I've had enough of you lot sneaking in here to see which list your child is on. Out with you. Out, right now!"

While Tasha smiled to think of Snowflake sneaking a peek at the List, she hurried out the

Library as quickly as she could, wanting to get as far away from the Naughty List as possible. A pit of worry bubbled ominously in her stomach.

She didn't know what was going on, but she was determined to find out.

The List Elf pushed her glasses up her nose and looked down curiously at the List. She frowned to see the flickering name, jumping from list to list.

"Interesting," she said to herself. "That's never happened before."

Chapter 12

Alabaster Explains it All

Despite being lost in thought, worrying about the list, Tasha trudged along the path, searching for her way back to the toy workshop. She passed the reindeer barn and the sleigh shed until, finally, she spotted the enormous toy workshop. Between them all stood Father Christmas's warm, welcoming house.

To her delight, the man himself stood there, on the steps up to his home, chatting to a small group of elves, his cheeks turned up in a bow. The beard on his chin was as white as snow and his eyes twinkled with the excitement of Christmas.

She sighed. Finally, after all she'd discovered at the North Pole village and all the adventures she'd had, *now* she could speak to Father Christmas himself.

She strode along the path heading straight for him. This was it. This was her moment. She was going to ask Father Christmas to grant her wish. She was ready.

Nothing would stop her.

"*What* are you *doing*?"

Blitz grabbed Tasha by the wrist and tugged her between the elf houses. His face was so puffy and cross he looked like he was about to explode.

"You're going to get us *both* in *big* trouble!" he raged, quietly, so no one would hear them. "You can't tell the boss you're here! That's the *worst* thing you could do!" He shook his head as if he couldn't believe anyone would be that foolish. "Are you trying to destroy Christmas?"

"No, of course not," Tasha snapped back. "What are you talking about? Why do you keep saying that? What is going on?"

"Look, come with me. I know someone who can explain it all."

They soon arrived at the strangest little elf house Tasha had seen yet. It was roughly the same shape as the other elf houses but it had a metal roof, where the other roofs were tiled or thatch.

Not only that! This house had a telescope poking out of the roof and wires leading everywhere, like very odd and not at all jolly bunting. Strange, bubbling, swirling noises were coming from inside.

"What's in there?" Tasha asked, feeling more than a little weary.

"Alabaster," said Blitz pushing open the front door

to the tinkle of a hidden bell.

"What's an alabaster?" She hesitated at the doorway.

"Well, come in and you'll find out."

Under no circumstances did Tasha want to go into that strange, little elf house. Her mind went wild picturing all the weird, awful and ultimately dangerous things that could be in there.

She dithered.

"Come on, *house elf,*" he grumbled, catching Tasha by the wrist and tugging her through.

She stumbled, tripping over the entrance. When she looked up, she gasped. She had never seen anything like it. Flasks and test tubes and beakers covered every surface and were even sitting all over the many piles of ancient, dusty books. The flasks glooped and gurgled and some even steamed. She could barely shimmy her way through all the different scientific equipment as she followed after the grumpy elf.

"What is this place?" she asked, drifting along behind Blitz. "It's like.. it's like.. I don't know what it's like!"

"This is Alabaster's place," he said, as if everyone knew that, "He'll be able to explain why you have to go home. Now."

None the wiser, Tasha made sure she stayed close to Blitz as she eyed the dangerously bubbling equipment wondering why on Earth it needed to be here, in the village at the North Pole. What were they cooking up?

They found the elf called Alabaster curled up in a tall chair beside the fireplace, gently snoring away. Blitz coughed. When Alabaster didn't move, he coughed again. He coughed so loud that he started coughing for real and Tasha had to fetch him a glass of water.

"Ah! Blitz Bookman! Just the chap. This is perfect!" exclaimed Alabaster, leaping up from his chair. He straightened the three points of his white hair and pushed his glasses up his nose.

Alabaster was a taller elf, thinner than most of the others and wore red and green dungarees under a messy, once-white lab coat. He shoved some red and white striped sweets into Blitz's hands. "I've invented the most curious sweetie and you're just the one to try it out! It's got a few odd quirks but, well, you've never wanted *all* your fingers, have you? Oh, it'll probably be fine."

"It's just Blitz now, Alabaster," Blitz reminded him, distractedly placing the curious sweets on a table. "I don't work on the List anymore. Listen, I've brought someone to see you."

"Two guests, oh how exciting. I think I have enough sweets for you both but-"

Alabaster froze when he saw Tasha and the smile drained from his face. He didn't move except for blinking, twice.

"Eee, gads!" he exploded, "A human! This is a disaster, this is terrible. This is a catastrophe!"

Tasha's face dropped and her heart sank. This wasn't good, it wasn't good at all. She stepped back, wishing she could disappear. This whole trip was turning out to be awful, worse than she could ever have imagined.

"A human, at the North Pole! It's our undoing. It's terrible. It's awful."

She thought about the List and how her name had flickered onto the Naughty List. Was that part of her undoing? Tasha was scared to ask.

Only after they'd given Alabaster a nice cup of tea and he'd had a good sit down did he actually seem calm enough to explain. He pulled a device from a drawer beside him and showed it to Tasha and Blitz.

"My old Naughty or Nice detector," he said, smiling with the memory. "I used to use it when I did deliveries."

Tasha gasped, again, "You used to deliver the presents with Father Christmas on Christmas Eve?"

He nodded. "I did, indeed. But that was when I was younger. I shall explain everything."

He pointed the Naughty and Nice detector at Tasha and squeezed the handle. Immediately, the detector blinked into life, flicking between green for naughty and golden for nice. Tasha realised this was just like the List. She bit her lip, begging the detector to choose Nice.

For one heart, wrenching moment, the light stayed on green for that little bit too long, before flicking back to gold for an equally long time.

"This is just what the list did," Tasha explained.

"What?"

"You've been to the List?" Blitz snapped. "I'm

going to be in so much trouble!"

"Why? What's going on?" Tasha searched their distraught faces for some answers.

"You're in flux," Alabaster explained, pointing to the flickering lights. "It can't decide if you've been naughty or nice."

"But I haven't been naughty!" Tasha exclaimed. "My mum doesn't even like that word!"

"You're at the North Pole!" Blitz cried, "You're not supposed to be here."

She hadn't thought of hitching a ride on the postal sleigh as being naughty, but maybe it was. Maybe she *was* naughty. She didn't like that idea at all.

"But, why is it naughty to be here?" she asked, hoping they'd say it wasn't.

"Oh, yes," said Alabaster, putting his detector down, "I've got a book about it here, somewhere. Wait there."

Dust billowed up all around them as Alabaster shuffled between the piles of books precariously balanced between test tubes and beakers.

"Ah-ha!" he cried, "Here it is."

As he sidled his way back, three beakers fell to the floor and smashed. Alabaster didn't notice but a purple foam spiralled out of the glass and escaped under a tablecloth. Tasha tried not to look at it.

"Here, see," said Alabaster, leaning over the book. "All the world's children must be asleep in their beds when Father Christmas delivers presents," he read, "It's all about the List. The magic is trying to look for you in your world but you're here, so the magic is in flux, bending around itself. It's all tangled up and getting in knots. This could destroy all the North Pole magic forever. It could destroy Christmas for everyone, everywhere."

Chapter 13

The Real Sleigh

Tasha didn't say anything. She hardly dared to breathe. Her ears were ringing and tears prickled at her eyes. It couldn't be true. It just couldn't. She couldn't bring about the end of Christmas for everyone everywhere forever! That was terrible!

Blitz looked from Tasha to the book, from the book to Alabaster as if he couldn't believe it either.

"Is that the right book?" he demanded. "I knew it was bad but... What can we do?"

Alabaster shook his head sadly. "It says here elves can't do anything to repair the damage." He looked at Tasha who quivered in the corner. "Only the human child can fix this."

Blitz slumped down in stunned horror.

Her mind was racing. She imagined all the children all over the world waking up on Christmas morning to find not a single toy under the tree. No Christmas sacks, no full stockings, nothing. And it was all her fault. She'd been so thoughtless. She'd been so selfish. *Billy would never make a mistake like this*, she thought to herself. Billy always did everything right.

"I'll go," she said quietly. "I'll go back to my house and never come back." She'd have to tell Billy she couldn't help him in his tournament. Things were going very wrong

Alabaster looked at her sadly. "I'm afraid it's too late. We need magic to fix this. Luckily, you came straight here so the damage should be easy to repair."

She looked up. "But.. we didn't come straight here."

"What do you mean?" Blitz and Alabaster asked at the same time.

"Well, I've been to the toy workshop, the candy kitchen, the Post Office –"

"The List!" Blitz cried in alarm.

"*The List*? This is a disaster!" wailed Alabaster. "We're going to need the most powerful Christmas magic there is. It's the only way to fix this before Christmas is destroyed forever."

"No!" Blitz gasped. "We can't!"

"Yes!"

"But.. no…"

"Definitely."

"Really?"

"Absolutely."

"Okay!"

"What?" Tasha cried, making no sense of either of them.

"We need magic from the star at the top of the Christmas tree," Alabaster declared.

She nodded. "Okay, where do we get that? Is it in a bottle somewhere?"

"It's at the top of the Christmas tree, of course," Alabaster explained. "It's the best place to keep it, nearest to the northern lights."

She was a little bit worried where this conversation was going. "So, who goes up there to get it?"

"It can only be you," Alabaster told her.

Tasha's stomach flipped.

Blitz said, "You're the only one who can climb the tree to get the magic and save the whole of Christmas."

"I can't climb the tree," said she flatly. She couldn't even climb the climbing wall at Billy's club and she never would if she didn't ask her wish and magic some bravery into her. "No, there has to be some other way. Don't you have magic in here? In your house?"

"This is the only way. We have to get the magic before Christmas Eve or no one will get any presents."

"Christmas will be destroyed," Alabaster added.

She shook her head. "No, it can't be! I can't do it!" She backed away, her heart pounding hard in her chest. Her throat went dry. "I can't. I can't climb the tree." *I'll fall,* she thought.

She fled from Alabaster's little elf home leaving Blitz and Alabaster far behind her. She dashed off towards the warm lights of the North Pole village heading for the sleigh shed and the reindeer barn.

If it meant ruining Christmas for all the children around the world, she would go home. It was simple. Her wish wasn't that important, not as important as Christmas. Even Billy would agree with that!

She made it to the reindeer barn in no time. Tears ran down her cheeks but she ignored them. She had things to do.

She wiggled her way through the half open door and into the cosy gloom of the reindeer barn. The air was musty with the smell of large animals and as Tasha's eyes grew used to the dark, she began to make out the shapes of enormous, powerful reindeer.

She had no idea how to hitch up a reindeer to a sleigh. She had no idea how to drive a sleigh. She had no idea how to get home but she knew she was going to try. If it meant saving Christmas for every child in the world, she *had* to try. Even if it meant not getting her Christmas wish. Guilt gripped her heart as she knew she was letting Billy down, but she couldn't ruin Christmas. She couldn't be the one to upset every kid in the whole world.

It didn't take Tasha long to find the trainee reindeer who'd driven the postal sleigh. He was the smallest of all the reindeer and his stall was right at the front of the barn. The trouble was, she noticed something different about the trainee reindeer, as she led him out his stall. The reindeer didn't shimmer with a golden light anymore and the sparkle in his eyes was gone, swapped with a dull gleam, like an ordinary reindeer.

She didn't have time to worry about it. She led the trainee reindeer next door to the sleigh shed and stopped statue still.

In the centre of the shed, illuminated by a golden light beaming down from the ceiling, was Father Christmas's sleigh. It was a bright, Christmas red with gold trims, everything Tasha had ever dreamed off. The seats had black velvet cushions and she spotted a golden hook where the reins for the reindeer would rest.

A shiver of excitement fizzed down Tasha's spine.

This was The Sleigh.

The *real* Sleigh.

It was amazing! It was fantastic! It was right in front of her and it was really real. She wished more than anything she could have a ride in Father Christmas's real sleigh. That would be a dream come true!

She shook her head. She didn't have time for sightseeing. She needed to get a move on. Tasha was about to destroy the whole of Christmas for everyone everywhere. She had to get home before Christmas Eve or all of Christmas would be *ruined*.

Chapter 14

Broken Magic All Around

Through trying lots of different ideas, that were all wrong, and dropping the harness painfully on her foot three times, Tasha finally managed to hitch the trainee reindeer up to the postal sleigh. She wasn't quite brave enough to take The Sleigh, Father Christmas's sleigh and besides, he needed it that night to deliver all the presents.

She clambered in, starting to feel a bit less worried and a lot more hopeful. Everything would be back to normal in the morning, she was sure of it.

"Go!" Tasha called to the trainee reindeer.

He didn't move. In fact, he acted as if he hadn't heard her.

"Let's go!" Tasha called again. "I need to get home. Please," she added. Mum always said 'a please never hurt'.

The reindeer didn't move a single muscle. It was as if the trainee didn't know what to do, but he'd flown the sleigh before! What was going on?

She clambered out of the postal sleigh and looked closely at the reindeer. Now that she was really paying attention, she had to admit he did look much less magical now, more like an ordinary, young reindeer. Her hope started to wobble but she wasn't going to give up, not yet.

"Maybe you just need some magic," she said to the trainee. "There must be some around here somewhere."

After an exhaustive search of the sleigh shed, Tasha had to agree, it didn't contain any magic at all. She did find spare parts, lots of tools and an ancient sleigh that looked as if it was falling apart but nothing that would help the trainee reindeer know how to pull a sleigh.

She was just about to return him to the barn and try a different reindeer when Blitz came bursting through the sleigh shed doors.

"There you are!" he cried. "We've been looking for you everywhere!"

Tasha said nothing and continued unhitching the trainee reindeer from the sleigh. It was even more complicated than hitching him on and it wasn't going very quickly.

"I've got to go home!" she blurted, her voice cracking. "I've ruined everything. Billy would never have made this mistake. I've got to get home before it's too late."

"I can see you're upset," said Blitz, "But we can work on this together. I'll help you."

"I don't need help," Tasha said firmly. "I *need* to go home."

That was when Blitz noticed the trainee reindeer.

"Hey, what's happened to Jingle?" he asked, rushing over. "And the postal sleigh. It's the magic," he cried, looking the sleigh over then peering into Jingle the reindeer's eyes. He threw his hands through his hair. "They've lost their magic! What did you do?" Blitz snapped at her.

"Do? I didn't *do* anything. I'm just trying to get home. Like you wanted," she added, pointedly.

"Oh. This is bad. This is really bad. If the reindeer can't fly then the sleigh won't fly and the presents won't be delivered and – oh! This is bad. This is so, so bad."

"We could try Father Christmas's sleigh?" she suggested.

Blitz rubbed his bearded chin. "It is the most magical vehicle in the entire North Pole. It'll *have* to be able to fly."

Blitz fetched Donner, a reindeer from the reindeer barn while Tasha got Father Christmas's sleigh ready. They hitched up the bigger, stronger, more magical reindeer then she clambered aboard the sleigh. She paused for a moment, excitement tingling with the fact that she was in *Father Christmas's real sleigh that he really used to deliver all the presents for real.* It was like living in a dream.

Blitz handed her the reigns. She took a deep breath, to calm her nerves, then shouted, "Go!"

Nothing happened.

Donner stomped his foot and looked around for some food.

"I think he says, 'Hee-ah!'" Blitz told her.

Tasha tried again. She took a firm hold of the reins and shouted, "Hee-ah!"

All of a sudden, magic swirled all around her. A golden sparkle of light glittered from the sleigh. Her hair lifted from her shoulders and a delightful tingle ran down her spine.

Excitement buzzed in Tasha stomach. She'd done it! She was finally going home. She felt a little pang of sadness that she wouldn't be able to ask her wish, but she was glad she'd be able to fix the magic for everyone.

Without warning, the light spluttered and went out. Tasha blinked in the gloom.

"Father Christmas's sleigh is broken!" Blitz cried in alarm. "This has never happened before! How will he deliver all his presents? Oh, this is so, so bad."

Chapter 15

Tasha and Snowflake

Tasha bolted out the sleigh shed, and ran as fast as she could, terrified she'd break something else. Turned around and lost, she found herself in a forest. Trees thick with dark, green leaves lined the path so densely she could hardly see through them.

At least here, in the forest, she couldn't break anything else, she thought to herself. Her mind raced with the broken sleigh, the reindeer who couldn't fly, all the children disappointed on Christmas morning when they didn't get any presents. This was all her fault. She was so angry with herself. She should have known human kids couldn't go to the North Pole, but how could she?

She felt like the baddie in her own story.

"Oh no, oh dear," said a familiar voice not too far off in the trees. "This is a disaster. It's awful. Oh dear, oh dear."

"Hello?" Tasha called out, worried what she'd find this time.

"Hello?" the voice called back. "Ah, it's the wandering house elf again. The house elf."

The friendly face of Marley smiled at Tasha as he pushed his way out through the trees. Despite his kind smile, he didn't look very happy. In fact, worry creased his brow and he wrung his hands.

"Is everything okay?"

"I'm afraid I don't have good news," Marley told her gravely. "Well, you can see for yourself. The Tinsel Forest."

Tasha looked around at the trees but couldn't see a tinsel tree anywhere. These trees were covered in pine needles, just like normal. Then, she realised. She was standing *in* the Tinsel Forest but, without North Pole magic, the tinsel trees were just ordinary trees with pine needles.

Her mouth dropped open in horror as her heart sank even deeper. It was getting worse and worse. She was breaking everything!

She ran from Marley through the North Pole village until she came upon the bright, warm lights of the canteen. She raced through the doors, desperate to see happy, jolly faces but what she found was the exact opposite.

All the elves, the snow people, fairies, nutcrackers and gingerbread people were frowning into their mugs. Mouldy cookies lay uneaten on the plates.

Instead of the sweet smelling deliciousness of the hot chocolate, the air was filled with the smell of rotten farts. By the looks on everyone's faces, it tasted that way too. Tasha had even broken the magic of the hot chocolate. This was the worst day of her life!

She ran, escaping from the canteen. She dashed out into the chill air of the North Pole village and stood gasping for breath. Her chest felt tight, she could hardly breathe. A sinking, sick feeling rose up from her stomach and swamped her. She *was* the baddie! *She* was the one destroying Christmas. She was ruining everything!

"Tasha?" someone said loudly. "Tasha, is that really you?"

Blinking away heavy tears, she gazed up into the concerned face of her house elf, Snowflake. Instead of being small enough to fit on a mantle piece, Snowflake was as tall as Tasha and wore almost the same outfit even down to the golden buttons.

"Snowflake!" Tasha cried, wrapping her arms around her house elf in a tight hug. She couldn't stop her tears from tumbling down her cheeks this time. "I've ruined everything! I need Billy's help. I can't do this by myself. I've destroyed Christmas!"

"Wait, what?"

"Ah, Snowflake," said Blitz, totally out of breath. "I see you've found our stowaway human."

"Blitz? How do *you* know Tasha?" asked Snowflake, sounding very confused. "You had both better tell me what's going on. Right now."

Between Blitz's embarrassed retelling and Tasha's sobs, Snowflake managed to hear the entire tale. She listened in silence, not wanting to interrupt the story even for questions. It wasn't until the tale was told that she leaned back and considered her options.

"That scarf," she said, lifting one end to get a better look. "That's Berry's scarf. You were the snow person near the bauble cars!"

"I'm so sorry!" Tasha wailed.

Snowflake sat back and stared, completely stunned. Tasha felt awful. Guilt thumped inside her heart and a strange, tight feeling gripped her chest.

"I just wanted to speak to Father Christmas and I didn't know it would break the sleigh and now all the magic at the North Pole is breaking and the tinsel trees are gone and the hot chocolate smells like farts and its all my fault and I wish there was something I could do but I think I've ruined Christmas!"

"Tasha," Snowflake said, "Come with me. I'll send you home through the house elf portal."

"But, hang on," Blitz tried but Snowflake and Tasha were already heading towards the House Elf Portal Station.

The Portal Station was tucked away at the back of the North Pole village where nothing could fall through by accident. The portals were surrounded by three layers of pretty, picket fencing painted in all the festive, Christmas colours. Tasha had to pass through four gates that Snowflake unlocked each time before she could even get close to the Portal Station.

Unfortunately, as they got closer, Snowflake's frown grew deeper and deeper.

"This isn't right," she muttered.

The portals were doorways, stood up in the snow

with little, peaked roofs over the top. Arranged in a semi-circle, their doorways were blank, wooden and plain.

"Is something wrong?" Tasha asked in a small voice. She dreaded the answer.

"These portals should be shimmering with gold and green," said Snowflake. She ran her hand down the first doorway. "It's just… wood." Snowflake snatched the door knob and, opening the door, saw only the snow on the other side. "This should be your house," Snowflake explained. "Here, on the other side of the door." She shut the door and opened it a few times before she could accept this too was broken. "This has never happened before."

"It's the broken magic," Tasha explained glumly. "Is there any other way to get me home?"

"I do have one more idea," said Snowflake, as Blitz caught up with them. "Let's all go to the Post Office."

Chapter 16

The North Pole Post Office

The Post Office was a disaster, just like everywhere else. Letters zoomed all over and none of the letters were being read because the elves were too busy ducking for cover. The sorting machine was spewing out envelops causing elves to dance around, trying to catch them. Tasha had to duck three times, as she stepped through the door, to avoid being bonked on the head by swarms of soaring letters.

"The magic is breaking in here too!" Blitz called over the rush of the storming letters.

"Quick," cried Snowflake. "Find the largest envelop you can. I'm going to write a letter."

"I'll find a stamp," Tasha shouted.

She felt a little better now, with Snowflake in charge. Tasha allowed herself a little hope. Nothing could go wrong with the best house elf in the whole North Pole helping her. Everything was going to be okay and she didn't need to climb that ridiculously enormous Christmas tree after all!

"Quick, get in!" Snowflake commanded as Blitz raced over with an envelope so huge, it was big enough for Tasha to lie down. She quickly clambered in.

None of the postal elves paid them any attention. They were all far too busy chasing down all the wayward letters zipping in wild clusters above their heads.

Snowflake squeezed in a letter and folded the envelope so Tasha could still see out of it.

"A letter from the North Pole," said Snowflake. "This should get you straight home, if the magic is still working."

It wasn't.

Even after Snowflake had stuck on the special, large stamp, nothing happened. In fact, the envelope started to rip where Tasha's toes were wriggling and the top peeled open.

"Ah. Well, that didn't work," Snowflake pointed out, putting her hands on her hips.

Not only that, but all the letters that were flitting through the air suddenly dropped heavily to the ground. The machine shut down. The air fell still. The silence was deafening. An elf standing next to Tasha nudged an envelope with his toe but it didn't so much as flutter.

"This is not good," said Blitz.

"We should leave," Snowflake said quickly. She helped Tasha out the envelope and the three of them hurried through the Post Office door as quickly as they could.

Tasha, Snowflake and Blitz stood outside, staring down at the snow, each one of them trying to come up with a plan. Tasha felt lost in a fog of hopelessness. She couldn't think of any ways to get home. The sleigh was grounded, the reindeer had forgotten how to fly, Snowflake's portal was broken and even the letters had all slumped to the ground.

She felt a pang of guilt for all the children waiting to read their replies from Father Christmas, only to receive nothing at all. And worse, no one was going to get any presents! Not if the sleigh was broken.

This was all Tasha's fault.

"Okay," said Snowflake suddenly. "I've got a plan. We need to go to the toy workshop."

"No!" Tasha shook her head. "I can't go there! That's the worst possible place. What if I break the magic there too? It's Christmas Eve tonight! *No one* will get any presents." She shook her head again. "No, I won't be the baddie in this story."

"It could be our last chance to get you home," said Blitz.

Tasha looked up at Snowflake who wore a look of determination. "I have a plan," she told Tasha. "But I need a toy aeroplane."

Chapter 17

Another Bad Idea

With his hands on his hips and a disappointed look on his face, Blitz said, "I knew this wouldn't work."

Snowflake tried pushing the toy aeroplane down the path again, in the hopes that it would start but it didn't even splutter. Wooden toy aeroplanes couldn't really fly, not without magic.

"You're trying to use magic," Blitz complained, "But the magic is broken."

"But what else can I do?" Snowflake snapped. "I can't exactly put her on a train back to England."

Tasha's worst nightmare had come true. Everyone was arguing. No one was building anything in the toy workshop. Instead, all the elves wandered about, looking lost and confused. It was all falling apart.

She felt awful. Her tummy was all twisted up inside and she felt sick. She stared at the floor, lost in her own, anxious thoughts. What was Billy going to say? Would he hate her for destroying Christmas?

Outside the workshop, an enormous crash rocked the ground. She was shaken from her thoughts as Snowflake and Blitz raced outside with Tasha following behind.

The bauble cable cars lay shattered across the ground, the moonlight glinting from the shiny debris.

Panic rushed up inside Tasha. She couldn't breathe.

"Tasha!" cried Alabaster, racing over to them. "Tasha, you've got to climb the Christmas tree up to the star. You've got to!"

"But, I can't!" She really couldn't. She was terrified! It was Billy who went to climbing lessons. *He* should have been the one here, not Tasha. He could have saved the North Pole. "Oh, if only I was like Billy," Tasha said to herself.

"Now stop that, right now," snapped Snowflake. "I don't want to hear any more. Natasha Snowfield, there is nothing you can't do when you put your mind to it. My good friend, the Tooth Fairy, said you almost spotted her when she came to get your tooth not long ago. You'd barely fallen asleep when she arrived. And I had to listen to the Easter Bunny grumbling that he couldn't put eggs out at your house because you were watching so closely. He'd had to wait in the bushes for ages, he said."

Tasha bit her lip. The Easter Bunny had been there the whole time!

"I have seen you do so many wonderful and amazing things. Billy is a lovely boy and a kind brother and you are an incredible young person and a kind sister." Snowflake smiled at Tasha. "Don't compare yourself to anyone. You are you and you're a wonderful-"

All of a sudden, Snowflake's smile fixed and she fell silent. Before Tasha's eyes, Snowflake's face changed completely so she looked more like the toy elf she was at Tasha's house. The elf even seemed to shrink a little.

Snowflake shook her head and was soon back to normal. "Oh, I don't know what happened there. I was suddenly dizzy."

With an awful feeling in the pit of her stomach, Tasha thought she knew what was happening.

"It's getting worse," said Blitz pointing.

He had spotted a small group of snowmen who thumped along under a lamppost. Their worried expressions froze and they slowly stopped moving. She ran over to help but she was too late, the friendly snowmen had turned into real snowmen. They froze on the spot.

"Snowflake, what's going on?" asked a gingerbread man, running over. As he got closer, he shrank down until he was the size of a gingerbread man biscuit, and flopped on the ground, lifeless.

She backed away. "I'm so sorry," she cried. "I'm really sorry."

Snowflake grabbed her arm. "Tasha, you've got to get the magic from the Christmas star," she insisted, "You've got to save the North Pole."

As she spoke, Snowflake shrank. She kept on shrinking, down to the size she was at Tasha's house, the size of a doll.

"But I'm scared," Tasha whimpered. "I'm not brave."

"Tasha, brave people get scared," shrinking Snowflake explained. "They're scared, but they do it anyway. That's real bravery. I know you can do it."

With that final word, the house elf flopped on the ground, doll sized with her gently smiling doll expression, just how she looked at Tasha's house. The elf was silent.

"Snowflake!" Tasha cried, and scooped up her elf. Tears began to tumble down her cheeks. "Snowflake." She squeezed her house elf tightly as the tears fell. "I'm so sorry. I'm so sorry for all of it."

She squeezed her eyes shut, letting the last of her sadness and fears escape. She had to make room in her heart for determination because now, she finally understood what she had to do.

She tucked her house elf into her pocket and took a deep breath. Wiping away her tears, Tasha strode towards the enormous Christmas tree in the centre of the North Pole village.

She knew she was brave, because she was absolutely terrified and she was going to save the North Pole anyway.

Chapter 18

The North Pole Christmas Tree

The Christmas tree towered over Tasha so high that she could barely see the star shining at the very top. Its glow of pure magic danced in the northern lights. That was where she was headed and she was not going to give up. She was going to save Christmas.

To her horror, she spotted the baubles dotted about the tree had started to fade and the pretty, twinkling lights flickered.

This wasn't good.

She took a deep breath.

A tall, flimsy ladder disappeared up into the lowest branches of the tree. That was her route. Now all she needed to do was go. The trouble was, her feet didn't want to move.

Blitz and Alabaster were stood behind her looking almost as worried as she was scared.

"You can do it, Tasha," Blitz told her.

"We believe in you," Alabaster said.

With doll-sized Snowflake tucked into her pocket, she was all set to go. There was just something holding her back.

"Will you wait for me?" she asked Blitz.

"Of course."

"And when I've got the star, I'll come back down again, with the star?"

Alabaster raised his hand. "Ah, no. I knew there was something I'd forgotten." He fished around in his bag. "The star is enormous, much bigger than an elf house. I don't think a team of ten construction elves could move it!" He chuckled to himself. "I have prepared ... this!"

From his bag, Alabaster pulled a stubby, wide glass bottle. In one end, it had a cork decorated with gold and gilt. It was exactly the sort of thing that looked like it should contain magic, but right now, was completely empty.

"Be careful with it," he told her as he delicately handed her the bottle. "It's the only one I've got."

She held it tightly in one hand, promising Alabaster and herself that she would keep it safe.

"And then, all we have to do is spread the star's magic all around the North Pole village and everything will be back to normal?" Tasha checked. "I'll get Snowflake back?"

Alabaster pushed his glasses up his nose. "I do believe so," he told her. "You could save Christmas."

That was all she needed to hear. Still swamped with guilt for being the bad guy in her story, she was relieved to hear she could also be the hero.

Summoning all her courage, she took a deep breath and headed towards the bottom of the ladder. It was just as she was nearing the bottom wrung that she spotted someone very jolly and very red moving about on the other side of the tree.

She peered through the branches to get a better look and who could she see but none other than Father Christmas himself! He must have come to check what was happening with the flickering Christmas tree lights. He was so close, Tasha only had to take a few steps to stand next to him.

"I could ask my wish," she said to herself. "I *could*."

But she didn't. She stood frozen, pinned to the spot, not knowing what to do.

This was her chance to speak to him. The moment she fixed the magic, she'd be sent home. She wouldn't get another chance like this. If she didn't speak to Father Christmas *now*, she never would. If her wish was granted, she'd be brave like Billy. She'd be able to climb the tree without feeling scared at all. She'd be able to help Billy in his tournament.

Tasha looked down at Snowflake tucked into her pocket, at her elf's blank, doll-like expression. That was when she knew, she had to do this by herself.

She took another deep breath. Her heart was thumping. Alabaster and Blitz believed in her. She was sure Snowflake believed in her too, if she could talk.

She took the first step up the ladder and up into the Christmas tree, leaving Father Christmas and her wish behind.

Billy wore a harness when he climbed the mountain wall, she remembered. More than ever, she wished she had a harness on now.

Deciding to take that first step was definitely the hardest part. Now that she was making her way up the ladder, she had already reached the lowest branches.

Despite the magic breaking, despite everything going wrong, she could still see magical sparkles in the tree flashing like lightning down the branches. It filled her with the hope that she might actually be able to fix this. Tasha could actually save Christmas.

Everyone was watching her.

Blitz and Alabaster were calling elves over and a crowd was gathering below as she climbed. She tried not to look down.

The Christmas tree stretched up for what felt like miles. Tasha climbed on even when her muscles ached. She had to save Christmas.

She climbed so high she couldn't see the ground anymore. Wisps of cloud hung in the air. Still, she climbed upwards.

The northern lights danced in beautiful patterns above her head. She kept on climbing.

She still felt scared. She was worried she'd fall but inside her, a small ball of bravery was growing in her chest. The higher she climbed, the bolder she felt.

Tasha was finally starting to believe that she could save Christmas when she slipped.

Chapter 19

The Star

Tasha didn't have time to scream. She slipped, falling back, thudding into the thick branch below her with a heavy, 'Oof.' All the wind was knocked out of her.

She rolled off – into thin air! Gasping for breath, she fell.

She grabbed wildly at the branches, clinging on as tightly as she could. She was scratched and the rough bark scraped her palms but she clung on.

With an enormous heave, she managed to pull herself up onto a thick branch where she caught her breath. The first thing she did was check her pocket. The bottle was okay. She tugged it out and inspected it for cracks but thankfully, it seemed to be all in one piece.

Gulping in deep breaths, trying to calm down, she safely pushed the bottle back into her pocket. Looking around, she noticed the broken branch where she'd fallen. She'd have to be more careful.

"Is everything alright up there?" called Blitz. She could barely hear him. His distant voice swept away on the breeze.

"I'm fine!" she called back, not daring to look down.

"What?"

"I said, I'm fine!" she roared, louder, with a glance in Blitz's direction.

As her stomach lurched, she wished she hadn't looked down. A falling, swirling dizziness washed over her and she felt sure she was going to fall again. Had she done the right thing climbing up here?

She clung on desperately to the branches around her until the feeling passed. She was safe, she told herself. She was brave. Everything would be okay.

She *had* to climb to the top of the tree. She had to collect the magic from the star and save Christmas. Tasha felt the bottle in her pocket, nodded and pulled herself to her feet.

"I can do this," she said, "I can save Christmas."

Reaching up with both her hands and feet, she began to climb. Up and up she went, through the branches with the gentle pine needles tickling her ears. The tree was so dense up here that she had to squeeze and push herself through. The branches were thinner so she had to be very careful where she put her feet.

To think, only a little while ago, Tasha had believed she was the baddie in this story but here she was, being the hero. What would Billy think of her now?

With one more squeeze through the branches, her head popped out into the night. Above her the northern lights danced and right in front of her sat the beaming star on top of the Christmas tree.

The star was so tall it seemed to stretch all the way to the northern lights above. Made of pure, shimmering golden light, the star beamed with hope and joy and a warmth that made Tasha imagine the cosy warmth of a fire after playing in the snow.

She gulped. This was a wonder, more breath taking than she could ever have thought.

Snowflake shifted in her pocket. Could it be the magic? Was the star bringing Snowflake back?

She quickly tugged at the bottle in her pocket. If she was going to save Snowflake and everyone else, she had to work fast. She yanked the bottle out her pocket so hard, it suddenly slipped through her fingers and tumbled down onto the tree.

Everything went into slow motion.

She gasped.

She reached for the bottle.

Snowflake fell out her pocket.

If the bottle broke, she had nothing else to carry the magic!

It slipped away from her fingers.

Her heart lurched.

It landed on the soft pine needles of the Christmas tree but it didn't stop there. The bottle rolled away, heading towards the edge of the branches.

It was going to fall over the edge!

She dived, watching in dismay as it rolled away.

She gazed in horror as the bottle disappeared over the edge of the branches.

She slid across the smooth tree after it. With no way to slow down, she'd disappear over the edge too.

She had to catch the bottle before it was lost forever. She had nothing else to carry the magic!

With her arm outstretched, reaching, Tasha slid off the end of the branches.

In a heartbeat, her fist closed around the bottle neck. She'd done it! She caught the bottle!

She was still sliding.

With her free hand, she tried to grab at the branches but she was going too fast and the branches were too smooth.

She was going to fall off the tree!

Suddenly, something tight and hard wrapped around her ankles. She jerked to a halt, swinging back into the tree with a thump. The ground loomed below her. She squeezed her eyes shut and her heartbeat thundered through her ears.

She was stuck.

Then something yanked hard on her ankle, lifting her back towards the star. Was this Christmas magic? Tasha thought. Did the star save her?

She was almost right.

Chapter 20

The Magic

"Snowflake?" Tasha panted, getting her breath back. She gazed up at her house elf in amazement. "But.. how?"

Back to her normal North Pole size, Snowflake stretched her arms and pulled strange expressions as she moved the muscles in her face. "It's the Star's magic," Snowflake explained between stretching. "Even the air next to the Star is charged with magic. You did the right thing bringing me with you. If I'd have stayed a doll much longer, I'd be stuck that way. Now we've saved each other."

"We have to get back! We have to save all the elves!" *And the snow people, and the gingerbread people,* she thought to herself, *the reindeer, the sleigh, all of Christmas!*

Snowflake gave Tasha a nod. "All that is left to do, is for you to collect the Star's magic," she said proudly.

She stood aside so Tasha could step up to the star, the bottle gripped tightly in her hand. Tasha didn't want to spill even the tiniest drop.

"How do I do this?" she asked. "Just.. scoop?"

Snowflake smiled and nodded.

Tasha took a deep breath and puffed out her chest. As if scooping from a waterfall, she thrust the bottle into the Star. Her hand tingled and shone with golden light. The flask filled with a flaxen shimmer that flowed around the inside of the flask like liquid. She gazed at it in awe. This was incredible. She was holding pure magic from the North Pole. It was all over her hands like golden paint. She could hardly believe this was real.

"Better pop the cork in," Snowflake suggested.

Tasha did just that, and secured the bottle safely in her pocket.

"Ready to go?" Snowflake asked.

Tasha stepped up to the edge of the branches and took one last look at the view. From the very top of the mountainous Christmas tree, she gazed out with wonder at the magical North Pole village spread out below. The village sparkled like a blanket of snow sprinkled with shimmering stars. The colourful houses were adorned with twinkling lights that danced merrily in the air.

Her eyes followed the winding paths lined with candy cane lamps, leading to cozy little homes that seemed to be straight out of a storybook.

In the distance, she spotted a group of reindeer munching on crunchy carrots, their antlers decorated with jingle bells.

As she prepared to climb down the tree and fix the magic, she knew she had an important task ahead. The North Pole magic might be broken, but its beauty and warmth still shone through. With determination in her eyes and a smile on her face, she took one last, magical look at the village before turning back to Snowflake, ready to bring the sparkle and enchantment of Christmas to the North Pole village once again.

She took a deep breath and told the house elf, "Ready."

Climbing down was a lot quicker than climbing up. Her feet seemed to find all the easy branches to stand on, even without trying. She was moving so quickly, Snowflake struggled to keep up.

When her feet touched the cobble stones on the ground beneath the tree, she finally let out a heavy sigh of relief. She'd done it! She'd actually done it! She'd climbed to the top of the North Pole Christmas tree. Who else could say that?

Alabaster, Blitz and the other elves rushed over to Tasha, all of them asking questions at the same time so fast she couldn't understand them. But when Snowflake stepped out the tree, red faced and out of breath, they all gasped in disbelief.

"It worked!" cried Alabaster. "I knew it would! This is marvellous, simply marvellous! Do you have the bottle?"

"Here it is." She quickly but carefully handed the flask over to Alabaster.

All the elves 'ooh'ed and 'aahh'ed at the magical liquid. It shone a mystical, golden light across all their fascinated faces.

"How interesting," said Alabaster, holding the bottle up to his face. He shook away his thoughts and blinked at the crowd. "Right, yes. We had better get to work. Quickly," he said to the others. "Quickly, take these."

He handed large test tubes to each elf who promptly pulled out the corks, holding them ready.

"Snowflake, you take this one. You can turn the house elves back from dolls into elves again," Alabaster said as he handed Snowflake one of the large test tubes and poured in some of the golden light.

Snowflake pushed in the cork then dashed off towards the house elves.

"Here, Marley," Alabaster said to Marley who was grinning at Tasha. "You take this back to the tinsel forest."

"Will do. Hello again, Tasha. Hello. Nice to see you. With those climbing skills, you'd certainly make a good forest elf," he told her with a nod to show he was serious. "A good forest elf, indeed."

She blushed.

"Foreman Merry, take this to the workshop."

Off ran Foreman Merry to the Toy Workshop, gears and cogs falling out her hair as she went.

"Ah, Head Chef Holly," said Alabaster.

When Tasha saw Head Chef Holly, she gasped. This was the nice elf who'd given her directions to Santa's house when she was in the candy kitchen. Poor Head Chef Holly was covered head to toe in bright, colourful icing. It was in her hair, dripping down her face, and her apron was covered from top to bottom in a thick layer of festive, green frosting. Icing and cake mixture even squelched in Holly's shoes.

Tasha gushed, "Oh, Head Chef Holly, I am so sorry. I didn't know. I've really messed up. I am so sorry."

The chef sighed at her. "Now, look here, young lady," she said firmly. "Don't you worry about the kitchen. We will have it set to rights in no time. You made a few mistakes, that's true. But! If you never make any mistakes, you will never learn. Mistakes help you grow. I can see you have grown a lot today, already." With a twinkle in her eye she added, "Well done."

When almost all the magic had been handed out, one last elf arrived to collect his test tube.

Tasha gulped.

"Ah, Chief Noel. Here.. er... here's your.. er.. magic." Alabaster's voice faltered at the sight of Chief Noel's stern expression. He certainly was not a jolly, old elf.

"I knew it," he snapped. "I knew something was strange about you. You're not an elf at all! You're a stowaway! You'll most certainly be on the Naughty List."

Her heart sank. After all this, she'd still be on the Naughty List?

"Now, Noel," said a deep voice behind her. "That wasn't very jolly of you. Remember, it's Christmas."

Her heart thundering inside her chest, Tasha slowly turned around.

Beaming down at her with a warm smile was Father Christmas himself. She paused for someone to interrupt or to snatch her away but nothing happened. This was it. This was her big moment. Finally.

Chapter 21

Father Christmas

"I am so sorry!" Tasha cried, tears prickling at her eyes. "Please don't put me on the Naughty List."

With a wink to Tasha, Father Christmas said to Chief Noel, "I would be most grateful if my Post Office was once more fully operational."

"Yes, Father Christmas," said Chief Noel, stiffly. "Of course, Father Christmas." Chief Noel started to head off in the direction of the Post Office when he paused and turned back. "I just thought, almost destroying Christmas was definitely a Naughty List offence."

"Quickly, please," said Father Christmas with a serious tone.

When Chief Noel was gone, Father Christmas told them, "He is incredibly good at his job, but he can be quite a stickler for the rules." Father Christmas winked again at Tasha. "Now, I do believe I have you four to thank for saving Christmas."

Alabaster, Blitz and Snowflake puffed out their chests proudly but Tasha didn't feel proud.

"It's all my fault it was broken in the first place!

I shouldn't have come here," Tasha moaned. Now that she was standing in front of the real Father Christmas for real, she felt as if her wish was the most unimportant thing anyone could have ever wished for. She couldn't even bring herself to ask him. All this worry and anguish had been for nothing.

"And, if I may ask, why did you come to the North Pole? I know you worked exceptionally hard to get here. Your costume is extraordinarily realistic," Father Christmas marvelled. "I'd almost believe you'd borrowed Snowflake's uniform."

Tasha blushed. She tried to find the words to explain what had been so important she'd almost destroyed Christmas to get it.

"I had a wish," she confessed.

"Ah yes, of course," Father Christmas remembered. "Of course, your wish is granted."

She glanced at Snowflake, looking confused. Snowflake looked back, equally as puzzled. "But.. I didn't ask it, yet."

Father Christmas smiled at her with a sparkle in his eye. "Tasha, you have never needed a magical creature to grant your wish. You had everything you needed to grant your wish for yourself. You are focused, you are determined and you are brave." He knelt down so that he was looking straight into her eyes over his half rimmed spectacles. "It took bravery to climb my Christmas tree. And a true, kind heart to want to save Christmas. Tasha, you were an incredible person before you ever arrived at the

North Pole. Now, it is *my* Christmas wish, that you should believe that too."

Father Christmas's words echoed around her mind. A proud smile burst onto her lips and she grinned at Blitz, Alabaster and Snowflake who were patting her on the shoulders and slapping her on the back.

"Could I use my wish for someone else?"

"Ah yes. A wish given contains almost as much magic as the Star! It is for your brother, Billy? He's been very good this year," Father Christmas said. "I think he should have a rather special gift."

"Billy asked me to ask you for an electric bike. One with a phone charger and a battery that lasts forever and reflective panels on the frame," she told him, remembering carefully.

"Ah, yes," said Father Christmas, nodding. "That would be rather special. In red, I suppose?"

"That's Billy's favourite colour!" she cried. "Of course you'd know that, you're Father Christmas." She rolled her eyes at herself.

"And now, my dear, I believe it is time you went home. Tonight will be Christmas Eve so I shall be quite busy."

Snowflake stepped forward smartly. "No problem, Father Christmas. I'll take her now."

"How wonderfully helpful of you, Snowflake, but I think on this occasion it would be appropriate to return Natasha to her home on the sleigh."

She blinked a few times as if she couldn't believe what she'd heard. "The ... The Sleigh?" she stammered. "The *actual* sleigh? Father Christmas's real sleigh? Wow. Gosh. Wow!"

Father Christmas chuckled to himself. "The barn elves are hitching the reindeer up now, I believe. Shall we make our way there?"

Tasha nodded, unable to speak because so many words were caught up in her throat. She wanted to say 'thank you'. She wanted to keep saying 'sorry' over and over as if the number of times she said it would rub out all the mistakes she'd made. She wanted to ask questions about how the sleigh worked and who trained the reindeer and how old the sleigh was and if the reindeer really ate carrots or if that was a myth, but all the words stuck in her throat as she followed Father Christmas through the North Pole village. They passed all the buildings and jolly elves waved at her and cheered. Some shouted, 'Well done!'

Tasha blushed but made sure she waved back.

When they arrived at the sleigh shed, Tasha took one last look at the North Pole village. She'd never see it again. She wanted to remember every detail, every shimmer and shine, every sparkle and glitter. She took a deep breath, breathing in all the smells of cooking and hot chocolate and the cool, wintery air. This was where Tasha had the biggest adventure of her life, and she wanted to remember it forever.

"Wait!" cried a voice from around the corner. Alabaster?

"Hang on!" shouted another, gruffer voice. Blitz?

"Wait for us!" yelled another voice. And then it

was a thunder of voices all shouting for Tasha to wait.

The crowd of elves, now much larger as the magic had restored all the elves to their correct sizes, raced towards the sleigh. Nutcrackers marched between them, snow people thumped along, their hats wobbling, and even elf-sized gingerbread people, who were no longer biscuits, all made their way to the sleigh shed. Tasha felt so relieved to see everyone their correct sizes and shapes, an enormous smile filled her cheeks.

"I hope you ... didn't think...." Blitz panted. "Hang on.. Catch my breath... Shouldn't run at my age." He bent over, gulping down air. Blitz straightened up, having caught his breath and said, "I hope you didn't think you were leaving without a goodbye."

"Certainly not!" Alabaster continued. "The human girl who saved Christmas. This one needs its own book! That reminds me: you should have this, to remember your adventure." He pressed into her hands the bottle she'd used to scoop the magic. It still glowed with golden magic as she slipped it into her pocket.

"Now, you won't forget us, will you?" asked the nutcracker who'd first spoken to Tasha.

"I don't think I ever could if I tried."

"And don't forget who you are," said Holly the head chef.

Tasha nodded, remembering how brave she was and all the adventures she'd had. She bit her lip as tears threatened at the corners of her eyes. Despite everything, she'd made some good friends at the North Pole.

"You will write, won't you?" Blitz checked. "Because, you know, I'll collect your letters."

"Ah, about that," said Father Christmas, interrupting.

"Oh no," Blitz grumbled, "I knew I'd get in trouble. What could be worse than being a postal elf?"

"Oi!" shouted a voice at the back.

"Not a barn elf, please, not a barn elf," Blitz muttered.

"Hey!" objected a barn elf. "It's a great job."

"Blitz," Father Christmas began sternly, "I can see you've worked exceptionally hard in the Post Office and you haven't made anything explode, which is commendable."

Blitz nodded in agreement.

"Blitz Bookman, I believe it is time you worked on The List once more."

"What? Really?" Blitz cried, jumping for joy. "This is amazing! It's incredible! I won't let you down, Father Christmas, I promise. I'll be the best Book Keeper Elf you've ever had!"

"I am sure of it."

Marley pushed his way to the front of the crowd. "This is for you," he said, handing Tasha some tinsel. "It's very rare, very rate. It almost never comes in this colour. Almost never! I picked it just for you, just for you, for you, because you were such a fantastic Forest Elf. Fantastic."

Marley handed her an iridescent string of tinsel.

It shimmered magically in the light, reflecting a rainbow of colour.

"Thank you!" she gasped. "It'll look amazing on the Christmas tree in my room."

After all the hugs had been hugged and all the goodbyes had been said, it was time for Tasha to leave. She looked at all the smiling faces, happy in her heart that she had managed to put the North Pole mostly back to normal. But above all, she was glad of the many friends she'd made along the way.

She took one, last lingering look. If these were her final moments in the North Pole, she wanted to hold them in her heart.

"Ready?" Father Christmas asked gently after a moment or two.

Tasha nodded, feeling a heavy sadness. Even though she knew leaving was the right thing to do, part of her wanted to stay. She waved to all her friends, who waved back until they couldn't see her anymore.

Inside the sleigh shed, magic had definitely returned to Father Christmas's sleigh. It took five elves to hold it down. The four reindeer hitched up to the front of the sleigh were dancing in the air, trying to pull away from the ground.

"Quickly, if you don't mind, sir," said one of the elves, his teeth gritted as he used all his strength to stop the sleigh from flying away.

She spotted the star's magic shimmering in a dust cloud around the reindeer's hooves as she climbed into the sleigh. Father Christmas followed in after her.

He took the reins in his large hands and nodded to the elves. They dived out the way, throwing open the shed doors as the reindeer took one gallop, and another, and the sleigh leapt up into the sky with a jolt.

The wind streamed through Tasha's curly hair. Father Christmas's long, snowy beard flapped around his face. In half a second, the North Pole village was far below them.

She'd never been so excited. A real sleigh ride. This was like nothing she'd ever imagined. The postal sleigh had been incredible but this was something else. This was Santa's Sleigh.

Then, suddenly, the sleigh clunked. The sound of scratching metal echoed into the night and snap. Something broke.

Chapter 22

One, Last Disaster

The sleigh wobbled. The reindeer bumped into each other.

"Ah," said Father Christmas thoughtfully. "Oh dear."

"What was that?" Tasha cried.

"Oh dear," said Father Christmas, again.

"Yes, you keep saying that," she complained.

He leaned over the side of the sleigh. "I believe we may have a small problem."

"What's happened?"

"The magic fuel has fallen off," he said.

"What?" she cried, wondering if anything else could go wrong.

"Yes, the broken North Pole magic must have worked its way into the joints. Unfortunately, we will run out of magic very shortly."

She could see he was right. The magical mist around the reindeer's hooves was starting to fade away.

"Are we going to crash?" she shrieked.

"I certainly hope not. But if we do not find some

magic soon, we will need to brace for landing," he said, wrestling with the reins, trying to stop the reindeer from careering into each other.

She searched the sleigh for spare fuel, for something magical, anything.

She looked at her hands, feeling hopeless. Everything was going wrong again. It didn't matter how brave she was, everything went wrong.

Tasha stopped. She looked at her hands again. They were still glowing golden with North Pole magic.

Holding up her hands to show Father Christmas, she declared, "I have magic! What do I do?"

"You must get the magic to the reindeer," Father Christmas called over the rushing air as the sleigh soared through the sky miles above the North Pole village.

"But, how do I get to the..." Her voice faded away. The only way to get to the reindeer was to shimmy along the harness.

"If you can get to the reindeer, I believe it should keep us going long enough for a safe landing."

She let out a sigh. Just looking at the harness as it rocked between the reindeer hundreds of meters above the North Pole village made her dizzy. The sleigh jerked this way and that as the reindeer ran blindly with the last of the magic swirling around their feet. Shimmying along the harness would make climbing the Christmas tree look easy!

Her heart was thundering but Father Christmas was right. She was brave and she was determined.

There was nothing she couldn't do. She was going to climb the harness.

She swung her leg over the front of the sleigh, then the other leg so she was sitting on the very front. She kept her balance as she slid down the sleigh landing perfectly on the harness. Steadying her nerves, she wobbled as the sleigh shook but clung on until she got her balance again.

She took deep breaths and did not look down. To avoid even a glimpse of the ground rushing past far below her, Tasha looked up into the sky to see the northern lights dancing all around them, like magic cheering her on.

Her heart hammering inside her chest, she let go of the sleigh and edged forward along the harness. Her hair whipped around her shoulders. The wind billowed through her costume sending the skirt flapping.

She reached out with one hand and grabbed the strap of one of the reindeer. Gripping it tightly, she pulled herself along until she was standing beside the back two reindeer. She was half way there already.

Carefully, she sprinkled each hoof with the magic from her hands.

The sleigh jerked to the side.

Tasha slipped.

She was dangling in mid air, holding on only by the reindeer's strap. Her legs were waggling out into the air. Nothing was below her except an endless landscape of white.

"Sorry!" Father Christmas called from his sleigh.

With a heave, she managed to clamber back up onto the harness. Her heart thundering in her chest, she clung on for dear life. The sooner she got this done the better.

Edging along slowly, trying not to think about how close she'd come to falling off the sleigh entirely, she sprinkled a little more magic onto the hooves of the front two reindeer before rushing back, very quickly, to the safety of the sleigh.

But it wasn't enough. They could stay in the air for now but they'd have to land, soon. Tasha didn't want to land, she didn't want to go back to the North Pole and ruin Christmas again. She needed to go home.

She had to think. She needed an idea. Where could she get more magic?

"Fly towards the Christmas tree!" Tasha cried. "I know where we can get more magic, enough to get me home. Enough to fix the North Pole forever!"

Father Christmas didn't look sure. "In this moment, there is enough magic for us to land safely. Or we have enough magic to get us to the Christmas tree, but I do not have enough magic to do both." He looked Tasha straight in the eye. "Are you certain your plan will work?"

She looked at her hands, which still shone with the little magic that was left. Determination filled her heart. She could do this!

"I'm certain. Fly to the Christmas Tree!" Then she added, "Please, if that's okay? Thank you," because

Tasha was determined *and* polite.

He pulled hard on the reins turning the sleigh sharply towards the tree. They were headed straight to the Star.

"Fly as close to the star as you can!" she shouted over the roar of the wind. They were flying so fast now, her hair danced and her uniform whipped around wildly.

This had to work. It just had to. If Tasha stayed at the North Pole much longer, who knew what trouble it would cause?

The star was getting closer and closer still. They were headed straight for it. For one, heart wrenching moment, she thought they were going to crash. At the last second, Father Christmas pulled on the reins and instead of colliding with the star, the side of the sleigh scrapped past it, filling that side and two of the reindeer with Christmas magic.

"Wonderful idea, Natasha!" Father Christmas cried. "However did you think of it?"

"It was Snowflake!" Tasha called back. "The Star turned Snowflake back into an elf without even touching it. I knew flying near the star would fill the sleigh with magic."

"Indeed it has, indeed it has," said Father Christmas. "Well done, Natasha! Wonderful thinking. I'll do one more pass, then we will have plenty of magic to get you safely home."

Of course, Father Christmas was completely correct. They had more than enough magic to fly her all the way home and get Father Christmas back in time for Christmas Eve night.

As she climbed out the sleigh onto the crunching frozen grass, she began to shiver for the first time that night. On the horizon, she saw the sun creeping into the sky as its golden light caused the stars to fade.

"Thank you," she said to Father Christmas. She didn't want this moment to end. "For everything."

He smiled at her. "Thank *you*, for saving Christmas."

Tasha looked back at her house and realised, all the doors were locked.

"Father Christmas," she began, "How am I going to –"

When she looked back, all trace of Father Christmas and his sleigh were gone.

Despite the lack of sleigh, she could see the warm, golden glow of Christmas magic. But where was it coming from? Glancing down, she saw… Her hands! She still had a tiny bit of magic left.

She held up her hand and, to her surprise, a portal appeared, like the one she'd stepped through to get on the postal sleigh. She walked through, straight into her bedroom and quickly got into her pyjamas. That was when she noticed the last sparkle of magic on her hand blink out.

Chapter 23

Christmas Eve

"Wake up! Wake up! Wake up!" Billy shouted as he shook Tasha wake.

"Ugh! What time is it?" she asked, pulling her duvet back over her head.

"Wake up time!" he cried. "You fell asleep again, you've missed the elves. It's Christmas Eve!"

He jumped onto her bed and poked her on the shoulder with his finger until she snapped at him.

"Stop poking me, or I'll ask Father Christmas to put your name on the Naughty List."

"Ha! Wouldn't happen," he told her, "I'm too good. Just the Good List for me."

She had to admit that was true. Even Father Christmas had said so.

"Did you ask him for my bike? Did you? Did you? Did you?"

She tugged her pillow over her head. "Go away. I'm tired!"

"Can't. Mum says you have to come down for breakfast before it's lunch. It's really almost lunch, you know."

She shot up in bed and swept her hair off her face. "What? Lunchtime already?" She jumped out of bed and reached for her clothes. The elf costume was still in a crumpled heap on the floor where she'd left it last night. "Nothing's ready. We haven't hung up our stockings with care, we haven't baked the cookies, we still need to buy mince pies. This is a disaster!"

"You didn't answer my question. Did you see Father Christmas last night?" Billy leaned in and whispered, "Did you ask your mysterious wish that you wouldn't even tell me about?"

Tasha smiled to herself. "Well," she began, "as it turned out, I didn't *need* to ask my wish."

Tasha told Billy everything while they ate their breakfast in the kitchen. He didn't ask many questions but he did look rather worried when she told him about the destroying-all-the-magic-at-the-North-Pole part and the ending-Christmas-forever part.

"Sounds like an interesting dream," said Dad as he took a munch out of his toast. He carried on scrolling through is phone.

"It does sound a bit like a dream," Billy admitted. "The coolest most incredible dream ever," he added.

She inspected her hands. The magic had all gone

but then she remembered she did have one thing she'd kept from the North Pole.

When Dad had gone out to work in the garden and Mum was washing her hair (something that took a long time and lots of complaining from Mum) Tasha called Billy into her room. She found the pockets in the elf costume and pulled out the bottle she'd used to hold the magic. It still shone slightly with golden light even though all the magic had gone.

She carefully placed the bottle in her brother's hands.

"Woah," he gasped. "It really was real. All of it."

Tasha nodded knowingly. "And this too." She pointed to the iridescent tinsel wrapped around her tree. "It's from the tinsel forest." She took a deep breath and knowing it was the truth, told her bother, "And now, I've got buckets full of bravery. I'm going to help you with your tournament!"

"Woah, you've had a real adventure," he gasped, then frowned. "Wait, what happened to Snowflake?"

She yelped, "Snowflake!"

She dashed back downstairs and raced into the living room only to stop and stare. There, sitting on the mantle piece above the fire as she always did was Snowflake, her house elf. She was doll sized, as she always was at Tasha's house, but something about the look in Snowflake's eye told Tasha she was happy to see her.

She scooped up her best friend and gave her the biggest hug.

"It wasn't all a dream," Tasha said to herself. "It really wasn't."

Christmas Eve went off without a hitch. The stockings were hung by the fireplace with care, a plate of mince pies and freshly baked cookies were placed on the hearth and Billy and Tasha were tucked up into their beds. Even Mum and Dad had an early night.

She slept through the entire night without waking up even once, so she missed seeing Father Christmas one last time. She didn't mind, though. She had all her amazing memories and she had Snowflake.

Both Billy and Tasha woke up bright and early on Christmas morning. After pestering Mum and Dad for half an hour, they all, finally, went downstairs to see the presents under the tree.

Mum and Dad were bleary eyed, yawning and talking about making a coffee when Tasha and Billy got stuck into opening presents.

In her stocking, Tasha found one gift that was different to the rest. It was in a small, red box with a tag that read 'Natasha' in no handwriting she recognised.

Inside she found a small bracelet with a golden star. The note read,

'If you have any plans to return to the North Pole, please be sure to wear this bracelet as this will protect the magic. Merry Christmas, S.'

Tasha couldn't believe it. One day, she could go back to the North Pole only this time, she'd take Billy.

The End.

If you enjoyed this book, the author would be
very grateful if you could leave a review.

SCAN ME

Not ready to end your journey with Tasha and the elves?

Explore a treasure trove of thrilling reading and writing escapades on the author's website, and guess what? The best news is, they're all absolutely free!

Unleash your imagination by downloading these activities and keep the adventure alive in the most exciting way possible!

SCAN ME

About The Author

Frances Wong

Frances Wong lives in the West Midlands with her husband and two children.

Frances has been a primary school teacher since 2005 and is passionate about early reading and early writing, enabling children to explore books and storytelling in a variety of ways.

Frances delights in indulging in a variety of activities when she's not immersed in writing. She enjoys long walks, discovering new National Trust places and, naturally, diving into a good book. Her favourite authors are BB Alston, Terry Pratchett and Jill Murphy.

Books By This Author

How Lexi Walker Almost Saved The World

A science fiction adventure for 9 - 12 year olds. Join Lexi as she learns to use her new powers to defeat evil in the galaxy.

Lexi Walker And The Secrets Of The Issak's Stave

Continue Lexi's adventure through the cosmos as she learns about the origin of her powers and defeats those who try to steal them.

Printed in Great Britain
by Amazon